The Fifth Column

AND FOUR STORIES
OF THE
SPANISH CIVIL WAR

Books by Ernest Hemingway

The
Fifth Column

and Four Stories
of the Spanish Civil War

ERNEST HEMINGWAY

CHARLES SCRIBNER'S SONS · NEW YORK

Printed in the United States of America
Library of Congress Catalog Card Number 70-182369
SBN 684-10238-2 (Trade cloth)
SBN 684-12723-7 (Trade paper, SL)

CONTENTS

The Fifth Column

The Fifth Column

ACT ONE · SCENE ONE

It is seven-thirty in the evening. A corridor on the first floor of the Hotel Florida in Madrid. There is a large white paper hand-printed sign on the door of Room 109 which reads, "Working, Do Not Disturb." TWO GIRLS *with* TWO SOLDIERS *in International Brigade uniform pass along the corridor. One of the* GIRLS *stops and looks at the sign.*

FIRST SOLDIER. Come on. We haven't got all night.
GIRL. What does it say?

[*The* OTHER COUPLE *have gone on down the corridor*]

SOLDIER. What does it matter what it says?
GIRL. No, read it to me. Be nice to me. Read to me in English.
SOLDIER. So that's what I'd draw. A literary one. The hell with it. I won't read it to you.
GIRL. You're not nice.
SOLDIER. I'm not supposed to be nice.

[*He stands off and looks at her unsteadily*]

Do I look nice? Do you know where I've just come from?
GIRL. I don't care where you come from. You all come from some place dreadful and you all go back there. All I asked you was to read me the sign. Come on then, if you won't.
SOLDIER. I'll read it to you. "Working. Do Not Disturb."

[*The* GIRL *laughs, a dry high, hard laugh*]

GIRL. I'll get me a sign like that too.

CURTAIN

3

ACT ONE · SCENE TWO

Curtain rises at once on Scene II. Interior of Room 109. There is a bed with a night table by it, two cretonne-covered chairs, a tall armoire with mirror, and a typewriter on another table. Beside the typewriter is a portable victrola. There is an electric heater which is glowing brightly, and a tall handsome blonde GIRL *is sitting in one of the chairs reading with her back to the lamp which is on the table beside the phonograph. Behind her are two large windows with their curtains drawn. There is a map of Madrid on the wall, and a* MAN *about thirty-five, wearing a leather jacket, corduroy trousers, and very muddy boots, is standing looking at it. Without looking up from her book, the girl, whose name is* DOROTHY BRIDGES, *says in a very cultivated voice:*

DOROTHY. Darling, there's one thing you really could do, and that's clean your boots before you come in here.

[*The man, whose name is* ROBERT PRESTON, *goes on looking at the map*]

And darling, don't you put your finger on it. It makes smudges.

[PRESTON *continues to look at the map*]

Darling, have you seen Philip?

PRESTON. Philip who?

DOROTHY. Our Philip.

PRESTON. [*Still looking at the map*] Our Philip was in Chicote's with that Moor that bit Rodgers, when I came up the Gran Via.

DOROTHY. Was he doing anything awful?

PRESTON. [*Still looking at the map*] Not yet.

DOROTHY. He will though. He's so full of life and good spirits.

PRESTON. The spirits are getting awfully bad at Chicote's.

DOROTHY. You make such dull jokes, darling. I wish Philip would come. I'm bored, darling.

PRESTON. Don't be a bored Vassar bitch.

DOROTHY. Don't call me names, please. I don't feel up to it

just now. And besides, I'm not typical Vassar. I didn't understand *anything* they taught me there.

PRESTON. Do you understand anything that's happening here?

DOROTHY. No, darling. I understand a little bit about University
City, but not too much. The Casa del Campo is a complete puz-
zle to me. And Usera—and Carabanchel. They're dreadful.

PRESTON. God, I wonder sometimes why I love you.

DOROTHY. I wonder why I love you, too, darling. I don't think
it's very sensible, really. It's just sort of a bad habit I've gotten
into. And Philip's so much more amusing, and so much *livelier.*

PRESTON. He's much livelier, all right. You know what he was
doing last night before they shut Chicote's? He had a cuspidor,
and he was going around blessing people out of it. You know,
sprinkling it on them. It was better than ten to one he'd get shot.

DOROTHY. But he never does. I wish he'd come.

PRESTON. He will. He'll be here as soon as Chicote's shuts.

[*There is a knock at the door*]

DOROTHY. It's Philip. Darling, it's Philip.

[*The door opens to admit the* MANAGER *of the hotel. He
is a dark, plump little man, who collects stamps, and
speaks extraordinary English*]

Oh, it's the Manager.

MANAGER. How're you, very well, Mr. Preston? How're you, all
right, Miss? I just come by see you have any little thing of any
kind of sort you don't want to eat. Everything all right, everybody absolutely comfortable?

DOROTHY. Everything's marvelous, now the heater's fixed.

MANAGER. With a heater always is continually trouble. Electricity is a science not yet dominated by the workers. Also, the
electrician drinks himself into a stupidity.

PRESTON. He didn't seem awfully bright, the electrician.

MANAGER. Is bright. But the drink. Always the drink. Then
rapidly the failing to concentrate on electricity.

PRESTON. Then why do you keep him on?

MANAGER. Is the electrician of the committee. Frankly re-
sembles a catastrophe. Is now in 113 drinking with Mr. Philip.

DOROTHY. [*Happily*] Then Philip's home.

MANAGER. Is more than home.

PRESTON. What do you mean?

MANAGER. Difficult to say before lady.

DOROTHY. Ring him up, darling.

PRESTON. I will not.

DOROTHY. Then I will.

[*She unhooks the telephone from the wall and says*]:

Ciento trece— Hello. Philip? No. Come and see *us*. Please. Yes. All right.

[*She hooks up the phone again*]

He's coming.

MANAGER. Highly preferable he does not come.

PRESTON. Is it that bad?

MANAGER. Is worse. Is an unbelievable.

DOROTHY. Philip's marvelous. He does go about with dreadful people though. Why does he, I wonder?

MANAGER. I come another time. Maybe perhaps if you receive too much of anything you unable to eat always very welcome in the house where family constantly hungry unable understand lack of food. Thank you to another time. Good-bye.

[*He goes out just before the arrival of* MR. PHILIP *nearly bumping into him in the hallway. Outside the door he is heard to say*]:

Good afternoon, Mr. Philip.

[*A deep voice says very jovially*]

PHILIP. Salud, Comrade Stamp Collector. Picked up any valuable new issues lately?

[*In a quiet voice*]

MANAGER. No, Mr. Philip. Is have people from very dull countries lately. Is a plague of five cent U. S. and three francs fifty French. Is needed comrades from New Zealand written to by air-mail.

PHILIP. Oh, they'll come. We're just in a dull epoch now. The shellings upset the tourist season. Be plenty of delegations when it slacks off again.

[*In a low non-joking voice*]

What's on your mind?

MANAGER. Always a little something.

PHILIP. Don't worry, That's all set.

MANAGER. Am worry a little just the same.

PHILIP. Take it easy.

MANAGER. You be careful, Mr. Philip.

[*In to the door comes* MR. PHILIP, *very large, very hearty, and wearing rubber boots*]

Salud, Comrade Bastard Preston. Salud Comrade Boredom Bridges. How are you comrades doing? Let me present an electrical comrade. Come in, Comrade Marconi. Don't stand out there.

[*A very small and quite drunken electrician, wearing soiled blue overalls, espadrilles, and a blue beret, comes in the door*]

ELECTRICIAN. Salud, Camaradas.

DOROTHY. Well. Yes. Salud.

PHILIP. And here's a Moorish comrade. You could say *the* Moorish comrade. Almost unique a Moorish comrade. She's awfully shy. Come in, Anita.

[*Enter a* MOORISH TART *from Cueta. She is very dark, but well built, kinky-haired and tough looking, and not at all shy*]

MOORISH TART. [*Defensively*] Salud, Camaradas.

PHILIP. This is the comrade that bit Vernon Rodgers that time. Laid him up for three weeks. Hell of a bite.

DOROTHY. Philip, darling, you couldn't just muzzle the comrade while she's here, could you?

MOORISH TART. Am insult.

PHILIP. The Moorish comrade learned English in Gibraltar.

Lovely place, Gibraltar. I had a most unusual experience there once.

PRESTON. Let's not hear about it.

PHILIP. You *are* gloomy, Preston. You haven't got the party line right on that. All that long-faced stuff is out, you know. We're practically in a period of jubilation now.

PRESTON. I wouldn't talk about things you know nothing about.

PHILIP. Well, I see nothing to be gloomy about. What about offering these comrades some sort of refreshment?

MOORISH TART. [*To* DOROTHY] You got nice place.

DOROTHY. So good of you to like it.

MOORISH TART. How you keep from be evacuate?

DOROTHY. Oh, I just stay on.

MOORISH TART. How you eat?

DOROTHY. Not always too well, but we bring in tinned things from Paris in the Embassy pouch.

MOORISH TART. You what, Embassy pouch?

DOROTHY. Tinned things, you know. *Civet lièvre. Foie gras.* We had some really delicious *Poulet de Bresse.* From Bureau's.

MOORISH TART. You make fun me?

DOROTHY. Oh, no. Of course not. I mean we eat those things.

MOORISH TART. I eat water soup.

[*She stares at* DOROTHY *belligerently*]

What's a matter? You no like way I look? You think you better than me?

DOROTHY. Of course not. I'm probably *much* worse. Preston will tell you I'm *infinitely* worse. But we don't have to be comparative, do we? I mean in war time and all that, and you know all working for the same cause.

MOORISH TART. I scratch you eyes out if you think that.

DOROTHY. [*Appealingly, but very languid*] Philip, *please* talk to your friends and make them happy.

PHILIP. Anita, listen to me.

MOORISH TART. O.K.

PHILIP. Anita. Dorothy here is a lovely woman——

MOORISH TART. No lovely woman this business.

ELECTRICIAN. [*Standing up*] *Camaradas me voy.*

DOROTHY. What does he say?

PRESTON. He says he's going.

PHILIP. Don't believe him. He always says that.

[*To* ELECTRICIAN]

Comrade, you must stay.

ELECTRICIAN.—*Camaradas entonces me quedo.*

DOROTHY. What?

PRESTON. He says he'll stay.

PHILIP. That's more like it, old man. You wouldn't rush off and leave us, would you, Marconi? No. An electrical comrade can be depended on to the last.

PRESTON. I thought it was a cobbler that stuck to the last.

DOROTHY. Darling, if you make jokes like that I'll leave you. I promise you.

MOORISH TART. Listen. All time talk. No time anything else. What we do here?

[*To* PHILIP]

You with me? Yes or no?

PHILIP. You put things so flatly, Anita.

MOORISH TART. Want a answer.

PHILIP. Well then, Anita, it must be in the negative.

MOORISH TART. What you mean? Take picture?

PRESTON. You see connection? Camera, take picture, negative? Charming, isn't it? She's so primitive.

MOORISH TART. What you mean take picture? You think me spy?

PHILIP. No, Anita. Please be reasonable. I just meant I wasn't with you any more. Not just now. I mean it's more or less off just for now.

MOORISH TART. No? You no with me?

PHILIP. No, my pretty one.

MOORISH TART. You with her?

[*Nodding toward* DOROTHY]

PHILIP. Possibly not.

DOROTHY. It *would* need a certain amount of discussion.

MOORISH TART. O.K. I scratch her eyes out.

[*She moves toward* DOROTHY]

ELECTRICIAN. *Camaradas, tengo que trabajar.*

DOROTHY. What does he say?

PRESTON. He says he must go to work.

PHILIP. Oh, don't pay attention to him. He gets these extraordinary ideas. It's an *idée fixe* he has.

ELECTRICIAN. *Camaradas, soy analfabético.*

PRESTON. He says he can't read or write.

PHILIP. Comrade, I mean, I mean, but really, you know, if we hadn't all gone to school we'd be in the same fix. Don't give it a thought, old man.

MOORISH TART. [*To* DOROTHY] O.K. I suppose, yes, all right. Downa hatch. Cheerio. Chin chin. Yes, O.K. Only one thing.

DOROTHY. But what, Anita.

MOORISH TART. You gotta take sign down.

DOROTHY. What sign?

MORISH TART. Sign outside door. All the time working, isn't fair.

DOROTHY. And I've had a sign like that on my room door ever since college and it's never meant a thing.

MOORISH TART. You take down?

PHILIP. Of course she'll take it down. Won't you, Dorothy?

DOROTHY. Certainly, I'll take it down.

PRESTON. You never do work anyway.

DOROTHY. No, darling. But I always mean to. And I am going to finish that *Cosmopolitan* article just as soon as I understand things the *least* bit better.

> [*There is a crash outside the window in the street, followed by an incoming whistling rush, and another crash. You hear pieces of brick and steel falling, and the tinkle of falling glass*]

PHILIP. They're shelling again.

> [*He says it very quietly and soberly*]

PRESTON. The bastards.

> [*He says it very bitterly and rather nervously*]

PHILIP. You'd best open your windows, Bridges, my girl. There aren't any more panes now and winter's coming, you know.

MOORISH TART. You take the sign down?

[DOROTHY *goes to the door and removes the sign, taking out the thumbtacks with a nail file. She hands it to* ANITA]

DOROTHY. You keep it. Here are the thumbtacks too.

[DOROTHY *goes to the electric light and switches it off. Then opens both the windows. There is a sound like a giant banjo twang and an incoming rush like an elevated train or a subway train coming toward you. Then a third great crash, this time followed by a shower of glass*]

MOORISH TART. You good comrade.

DOROTHY. No. I'm not, but I would like to be.

MOORISH TART. You O.K. with me.

[*They are standing side by side in the light that comes in from the open door into the corridor*]

PHILIP. Having them open saved them from the concussion that time. You can hear the shells leave the battery. Listen for the next one.

PRESTON. I hate these damned night shellings.

DOROTHY. How long did the last one go on?

PHILIP. Just over an hour.

MOORISH TART. Dorothy, you think we better go in cave?

[*There is another banjo twang—a moment of quiet and then a great incoming rush, this time much closer, and at the crashing burst, the room fills with smoke and brick dust*]

PRESTON. The hell with it. I'm going down below.

PHILIP. This room has an excellent angle, really. I mean it. I could show you from the street.

DOROTHY. I think I'll just stay here. It doesn't make any difference where you wait for it.

ELECTRICAN. *Camaradas, no hay luz!*

[*He says this in a loud and almost prophetic voice, suddenly standing up and opening his arms wide*]

PHILIP. He says there isn't any light. You know the old boy is getting to be rather terrific. Like an electrical Greek chorus. Or a Greek electrical chorus.

PRESTON. I'm going to get out of here.

DOROTHY. Then, darling, will you take Anita and the electrician with you?

PRESTON. Come on.

[*They go as the next shell comes. The next shell is really something*]

DOROTHY. [*As they stand listening to the clattering of the brick and glass after the burst*] Philip, is the angle really safe?

PHILIP. It's as good here as anywhere. Really. Safe's not quite the word; but safety's hardly a thing people go in for any more.

DOROTHY. I feel safe with you.

PHILIP. Try to check that. That's a terrible phrase.

DOROTHY. But I can't help it.

PHILIP. Try very hard. That's a good girl.

[*He goes to the phonograph and puts on the Chopin Mazurka in C Minor, Opus 33, No. 4. They are listening to the music in the light from the glow of the electric heater*]

PHILIP. It's very thin and very old fashioned, but it's very beautiful.

[*Then comes the heavy banjo whang of the guns firing from Garabitas Hill. It whishes in with a roar and bursts in the street outside the window, making a bright flash through the window*]

DOROTHY. Oh darling, darling, darling.

PHILIP. [*Holding her*] Couldn't you use some other term? I've heard you call so many people that.

[*You hear the clanging of an ambulance. Then in the quiet the phonograph goes on playing the Mazurka as the ——*]

CURTAIN COMES DOWN

ACT ONE · SCENE THREE

Rooms 109 and 110 in the Hotel Florida. The windows are open and sunlight is pouring in. There is an open door between them and over this door has been tacked, to the framework of the door, a large war poster so that when the door opens the open doorway is blocked by this poster. Still the door can open. It is open now, and the poster is like a large paper screen between the two rooms. There is a space perhaps two feet high between the bottom of the poster and the floor. In the bed in 109 DOROTHY BRIDGES *is asleep. In the bed in* 110 PHILIP RAWLINGS *is sitting up looking out of the window. Through the window comes the sound of a man crying the daily papers. "El Sol! Libertad! El A.B.C. de Hoy!" There is a sound of a motor horn passing and then the distant clatter of machine-gun fire.* PHILIP *reaches for the telephone.*

PHILIP. Send up the morning papers, please. Yes. All of them.

[*He looks around the room and then out of the window. He looks at the war poster which shows transparent across the doorway in the bright morning sunlight.*]

No.

[*Shakes his head*]

Don't like it. Too early in the morning.

[*There is a knock at the door*]

Adelante.

[*There is another knock*]

Come in. Come in!

[*The door opens. It is the* MANAGER *holding the papers in his hands*]

MANAGER. Good morning, Mr. Philip. Thank you very much. Good morning to you all right. Terrible things last night, eh?
PHILIP. Terrible things every night. Frightful.

[*He grins*]

Let's see the papers.
MANAGER. They tell me the bad news from the Asturias. Is almost finish there.

PHILIP. [*Looking at the papers*] Not in here though.

MANAGER. No, but I know *you* know.

PHILIP. Quite. I say, when did I get this room?

MANAGER. You don't remember, Mr. Philip? You don't remember last night?

PHILIP. No. Can't say I do. Mention something and see if I recall it.

MANAGER. [*In really horrified tones*] You don't remember, really?

PHILIP. [*Cheerily*] Not a thing. Little bombardment early in the evening. Chicote's. Yes. Brought Anita around for a little spot of good clean fun. No difficulty with her, I hope?

MANAGER. [*Shaking his head*] No. No. Not with Anita. Mr. Philip, you don't remember about Mr. Preston?

PHILIP. No. What was the gloomy beggar up to? Not suicide, I hope.

MANAGER. You unremember throw him out in street?

PHILIP. From here?

[*He looks from the bed out toward the window*]

Any sign of him below?

MANAGER. No, from entry when you coming in from Ministerio very late last night after go for communiqué.

PHILIP. Hurt him?

MANAGER. Stitches. Some stitches.

PHILIP. Why didn't you stop it? Why do you permit that sort of thing in a decent hotel?

MANAGER. Then you take his room.

[*Sadly and reprovingly*]

Mr. Philip. Mr. Philip.

PHILIP. [*Very cheerily, but slightly baffled*] It's a lovely day though, isn't it?

MANAGER. Oh yes, is a superbly day. A day for picnics in the country.

PHILIP. And what did Preston do? He's very well set up, you know. And so gloomy. Must have put up quite a struggle.

MANAGER. He in other room now.

PHILIP. Where?

MANAGER. One thirteen. Your old room.

PHILIP. And I'm here?

MANAGER. Yes, Mr. Philip.

PHILIP. And what's that horrible thing?

[*Looking at the transparent poster between the doors*]

MANAGER. Is a patriotic poster very beautiful. Has fine senti-
ment, only see backwards from here.

PHILIP. And what's it cover? Where's that lead to?

MANAGER. To lady's room, Mr. Philip. Now you have a suite of
rooms just newly married happy couple I come see everything
all right you need anything at all anyway ring and ask for me.
Congratulations, Mr. Philip. More than congratulations absolutely.

PHILIP. Does the door bolt on this side?

MANAGER. Absolutely, Mr. Philip.

PHILIP. Then bolt it and get out and have them bring me some
coffee.

MANAGER. Yes, sir, Mr. Philip. Don't be cross on beautiful day
like this.

[*Then hurriedly*]

Please, Mr. Philip, also remember food situation Madrid; if by
any chance too much food any kind including anything any little
can any sort always at home demanding lack every sort. In a
family now is seven peoples including, Mr. Philip you would
not believe what I permit myself the luxury of, a mother-in-law.
Everything she eats. Everything agrees with *her*. Also one son
seventeen formerly a champion of natation. What you call it the
breast stroke. Built like this——

[*He gestures to show an enormous chest and arms*]

Is eat? Mr. Philip you *cannot* believe. Is a champion also of the
eating. You should see. That is only two of the seven.

PHILIP. I'll see what I can get. Have to get it from my room.
If any calls come have them ring me here.

MANAGER. Thank you, Mr. Philip. You have a heart big as the
street. Is outside to see you two comrades.

PHILIP. Tell them to come in.

[*All this time* DOROTHY BRIDGES, *in the other room, is sleeping soundly. She did not awaken during the first of the conversation between* PHILIP *and the* MANAGER, *but only stirred a little in the bed. Now that the door is closed and bolted nothing can be heard between the two rooms*]
[*Enter* TWO COMRADES *in I.B. uniform*]

FIRST COMRADE. All right. He got away.

PHILIP. What do you mean he got away?

FIRST COMRADE. He's gone, that's all.

PHILIP. [*Very quickly*] How?

FIRST COMRADE. You tell me how.

PHILIP. Let's not have any of that.

[*Turning to the* SECOND COMRADE, *in a very dry voice*]

What about it?

SECOND COMRADE. He's gone.

PHILIP. And where were you?

SECOND COMRADE. Between the elevator and the stairs.

PHILIP. [*To* FIRST COMRADE] And you?

FIRST COMRADE. Outside the door all night.

PHILIP. And what time did you leave those posts?

FIRST COMRADE. Not at all.

PHILIP. Better think it over. You know what you're risking, don't you?

FIRST COMRADE. I am very sorry, but he's gone and that's all there is to it.

PHILIP. Oh no, it's not, my boy.

[*He takes down the telephone and calls a number*]

Noventa y siete zero zero zero. Yes. Antonio? Please. Yes. He's not there yet? No. Send over to pick up two men please in room one thirteen at the Hotel Florida. Yes. Please. Yes.

[*He hangs up the telephone*]

FIRST COMRADE. And all we ever did——

PHILIP. Take your time. You're going to need a very good story indeed.

FIRST COMRADE. There isn't any story except what I told you.

PHILIP. Take your time. Don't be rushed. Just sit down and think it over. Remember you had him here in this hotel. Where he couldn't get past you.

[*He reads in the papers. The* TWO COMRADES *stand there glumly*]
[*Without looking at them*]

Sit down. Make yourselves comfortable.

SECOND COMRADE. Comrade, we——

PHILIP. [*Without looking at him*] Don't use that word.

[*The* TWO COMRADES *look at each other*]

FIRST COMRADE. Comrade——

PHILIP. [*Discarding a paper and taking up another*] I told you not to use that word. It doesn't sound good in your mouth.

FIRST COMRADE. Comrade Commissar, we want to say——

PHILIP. Save it.

FIRST COMRADE. Comrade Commissar, you must listen to me.

PHILIP. I'll listen to you later. Don't you worry, my lad. I listen to you. When you came in here you sounded snotty enough.

FIRST COMRADE. Comrade Commissar, please listen to me. I want to tell you.

PHILIP. You let a man get away that I wanted. You let a man get away that I needed. You let a man get away who is going to kill.

FIRST COMRADE. Comrade Commissar, please——

PHILIP. Please, that's a funny word to hear in a soldier's mouth.

FIRST COMRADE. I am not a soldier by profession.

PHILIP. When you put the uniform on you're a soldier.

FIRST COMRADE. I came to fight for an ideal.

PHILIP. That's awfully pretty. Now let me tell you something. You come to fight for an ideal say, and you get scared in an attack. You don't like the noise or something, and people get killed—and you don't like the look of it—and you get afraid to die—and you shoot yourself in the hand or foot to get the hell out of it because you can't stand it. Well you get shot for that and your ideal isn't going to save you, brother.

FIRST COMRADE. But I fought well. I wasn't any self-inflicted wound.

PHILIP. I never said you were. I was just trying to explain something to you. But I don't seem to make myself clear. I'm thinking, you see, what the man is going to do that you let get away, and how I'm going to get him in a nice fine place like that again before he kills somebody. You see I needed him very much and very much alive. And you let him go.

FIRST COMRADE. Comrade Commissar, if you do not believe me——

PHILIP. No, I don't believe you and I'm not a Commissar. I'm a policeman. I don't believe anything I hear and very little of what I see. What do you mean, believe you? Listen. You're out of luck. I have to try to find out if you did it on purpose. I don't look forward to that.

[*He pours himself a drink*]

And if you're smart you won't look forward to it either. And if you didn't do it on purpose the effect is just the same. There's only one thing about duty. You have to do it. And there's only one thing about orders. THEY ARE TO BE OBEYED. I could, given enough time, explain to you that discipline is kindness, but then, I don't explain things very well.

FIRST COMRADE. Please, Comrade Commissar——

PHILIP. Use that word once more and you'll irritate me.

FIRST COMRADE. Comrade Commissar.

PHILIP. Shut up. I haven't any manners—see? I have to use them so much I get tired of them. And they bore me. I have to talk to you in front of my boss. And cut out the Commissar part. I'm a cop. What you tell me now doesn't mean anything. You see it's my ass too, you know. If you didn't do it on purpose I wouldn't worry too much. I just have to know, you see. I tell you what. If you didn't do it on purpose I'll split it with you.

[*There is a knock at the door*]
Adelante.

[*The door opens and shows two* ASSAULT GUARDS *in blue uniforms, flat caps, with rifles*]

FIRST GUARD. *A sus órdenes mi comandante.*

PHILIP. Take these two men over to Seguridad. I'll be by later to talk to them.

FIRST GUARD. *A sus órdenes.*

> [*The* SECOND COMRADE *starts for the door. The* ASSAULT GUARD *runs his hands up and down his flanks to see if he is armed*]

PHILIP. They're both armed. Disarm them and take them along.

> [*To the* TWO COMRADES]

Good luck.

> [*He says this sarcastically*]

Hope you come out fine.

> [*The four go out, and you hear them going down in the hall. In the other room,* DOROTHY BRIDGES *stirs in bed, wakes, yawns, and stretching, reaches up for the bell that hangs by the bed. You hear the bell ring.* PHILIP *hears it ring too. There is a knock on his door*]

PHILIP. *Adelante.*

> [*It is the* MANAGER, *very upset*]

MANAGER. Is arrest two Comrades.

PHILIP. Very bad Comrades. One anyway. Other may be perfectly all right.

MANAGER. Mr. Philip is too much happening near you right now. I tell you as friend. Try and keep a things quieter. Is no good come with so much happen all the time.

PHILIP. No. I guess not. And it's a pretty day too, isn't it? Or isn't it?

MANAGER. I tell you what you should do. You should make a day like this excursion and picnic in the country.

> [*In the next room* DOROTHY BRIDGES *has put on dressing gown and slippers. She disappears into the bathroom, and when she comes out she is brushing her hair. Her hair is very beautiful and she sits on the bed, in front of the*

*electric heater, brushing it. With no make-up on she looks
very young. She rings the bell again, and a* MAID *opens the
door. She is a little old woman of about sixty in a blue
blouse and apron*]

MAID. [PETRA] *Se puede?*
DOROTHY. Good morning, Petra.
PETRA. *Buenos dias, Señorita.*

[DOROTHY *gets into bed and* PETRA *puts the breakfast
tray down on the bed*]

DOROTHY. Petra, aren't there any eggs?
PETRA. No, Señorita.
DOROTHY. Is your mother better, Petra?
PETRA. No, Señorita.
DOROTHY. Have you had any breakfast, Petra?
PETRA. No, Señorita.
DOROTHY. Get a cup and have some of this coffee right away.
Hurry.
PETRA. I'll take some when you're through, Señorita. Was the
bombardment very bad here last night?
DOROTHY. Oh, it was *lovely.*
PETRA. Señorita, you say such dreadful things.
DOROTHY. No, but Petra it *was* lovely.
PETRA. In Progresso, in my quarter, there were six killed in one
floor. This morning they were taking them out and all the glass
gone in the street. There won't be any more glass this winter.
DOROTHY. Here there wasn't *any one* killed.
PETRA. Is the Señor ready for his breakfast?
DOROTHY. The Señor isn't here any more.
PETRA. He has gone to the front?
DOROTHY. Oh, no. He never goes to the front. He just writes
about it. There's *another* Señor here.
PETRA. [*Sadly*] Who, Señorita?
DOROTHY. [*Happily*] Mr. Philip.
PETRA. Oh, Señorita. How *terrible.*

[*She goes out crying*]

DOROTHY. [*Calling after her*] Petra. Oh, Petra!
PETRA. [*Resignedly*] Yes, Señorita.

DOROTHY. [*Happily*] See if Mr. Philip's up.
PETRA. Yes, Señorita.

[PETRA *comes to* MR. PHILIP'S *door and knocks*]

PHILIP. Come in.
PETRA. The Señorita asks me to see if you are up.
PHILIP. No.
PETRA. [*At the other door*] The Señor says he's not up.
DOROTHY. Tell him to come and have some breakfast, Petra, please.
PETRA. [*At the other door*] The Señorita asks you to come and have some breakfast, but there is very little as there is.
PHILIP. Tell the Señorita that I never eat breakfast.
PETRA. [*At the other door*] He says he never eats breakfast. But I know he eats more breakfast than three people.
DOROTHY. Petra, he's *so* difficult. Just ask him not to be stupid and come in here please.
PETRA. [*At the other door*] She says come.
PHILIP. What a word. What a word.

[*He puts on a dressing gown and slippers*]

These are rather small. Must be Preston's. Nice robe though. Might offer to buy it from him.

[*He gathers up the papers, opens the door and goes into the other room, knocking as he pushes the door open*]

DOROTHY. Come in. Oh, here you are.
PHILIP. Isn't this all very rather unconventional?
DOROTHY. Philip, you stupid darling. Where have you been?
PHILIP. In a very strange room.
DOROTHY. How did you get there?
PHILIP. No idea.
DOROTHY. Don't you remember *anything?*
PHILIP. I recall some muck about chucking someone out.
DOROTHY. That was *Preston.*
PHILIP. Really?
DOROTHY. Yes *very* really.
PHILIP. We must get him back. Shouldn't be rude that way.
DOROTHY. Oh, no. Philip. No. He's gone for good.

PHILIP. Awful phrase; for good.

DOROTHY. [*Determinedly*] For good and all.

PHILIP. Even worse phrase. Gives me the horrorous.

DOROTHY. What are the horrorous, darling?

PHILIP. Sort of super horrors. You know. Now you see them. Now you don't. Watch for them to go around the corner.

DOROTHY. You haven't had them?

PHILIP. Oh, yes. I've had everything. Worst I remember was a file of marines. Used to come into the room suddenly.

DOROTHY. Philip, sit here.

[PHILIP *sit downs on the bed very gingerly*]

Philip, you must promise me something. You won't just go on drinking and not have any aim in life and not do anything real? You aren't just going to be a Madrid playboy are you?

PHILIP. A *Madrid* playboy?

DOROTHY. Yes. Around Chicote's. And the Miami. And the embassies and the Ministerio and Vernon Rodgers' flat and that dreadful Anita. Though the embassies are really the worst. Philip, you *aren't*, are you?

PHILIP. What else is there?

DOROTHY. There's everything. You could do something serious and decent. You could do something brave and calm and good. You know what will happen if you keep on just crawling around from bar to bar and going with those dreadful people? You'll be shot. A man was shot the other night in Chicote's. It was terrible.

PHILIP. Any one we know?

DOROTHY. No. Just a poor man who was squirting every one with a flit gun. He didn't mean any harm. And some one took offense and shot him. I saw it and it was *very* depressing. They shot him very suddenly and he lay on his back and his face was very gray and he'd been so gay just a little while before. They kept every one there for two hours, and the police smelt of everybody's pistol and they wouldn't serve any more drinks. They didn't cover him up and we had to go and show our papers to a man at a table just beside where he was and it was *very* depressing, Philip. And he had such dirty hose and his shoes were completely worn through on the bottoms and he had *no* undershirt at *all*.

PHILIP. Poor chap. You know the stuff they drink is absolutely poison now. Makes people quite mad.

DOROTHY. But Philip, *you* don't have to be like that. And *you* don't have to go around and maybe have people *shoot* at you. You could do something *political* or something *military* and fine.

PHILIP. Don't tempt me. Don't make me ambitious.

[*He pauses*]

Don't open vistas.

DOROTHY. That was a dreadful thing you did the other night with the spittoon. Trying to provoke trouble there in Chicote's. Simply trying to *provoke* it, everybody said.

PHILIP. And who was I provoking?

DOROTHY. I don't know. What does it matter who? You shouldn't be provoking *anybody*.

PHILIP. No, I suppose not. It probably comes soon enough without provoking it.

DOROTHY. Don't talk pessimistically, darling, when we've just started our life together.

PHILIP. Our——?

DOROTHY. Our life together. Philip, don't you want to have a long, happy, quiet life at some place like Saint-Tropez or, you know, some place like Saint-Tropez *was* and have long walks, and go swimming and have children and be happy and everything? I mean really. Don't you want all this to end? I mean you know, war and revolution?

PHILIP. And will we have the *Continental Daily Mail* for breakfast and *brioches* and fresh strawberry jam?

DOROTHY. Darling, we'll have *œufs au jambon* and you can have the *Morning Post* if you like. And every one will say Messieur-Dame.

PHILIP. The *Morning Post*'s just stopped publishing.

DOROTHY. Oh, Philip, you're so depressing. I wanted us to have *such* a happy life. Don't you want children? They can play in the Luxembourg and roll hoops and sail boats.

PHILIP. And you can show them on a map. You know; on a

globe even. "Children"; we'll call the boy Derek, worst name I know. You can say, "Derek. That's the Wangpoo. Now follow my finger and I'll show you where Daddy is." And Derek will say, "Yes, Mummy. Have I ever seen Daddy?"

DOROTHY. Oh, no. It won't be like that. We'll just live somewhere where it's lovely and you'll write.

PHILIP. What?

DOROTHY. Whatever you like. Novels and articles and a book on this war perhaps.

PHILIP. Be a pretty book. Might make it with—with—you know—illustrations.

DOROTHY. Or you could study and write a book on politics. Books on politics sell *forever,* some one told me.

PHILIP. [*Ringing the bell*] I imagine.

DOROTHY. You could study and write a book on dialectics. There's *always* a market for a new book on dialectics.

PHILIP. Really?

DOROTHY. But, darling Philip, the first thing is for you to start here now and do something worth doing and stop this absolutely *utter* playboy business.

PHILIP. I read it in a book, but I never really knew about it. Is it true that the first thing an American woman does is try to get the man she's interested in to give up something? You know, boozing about, or smoking Virginia cigarettes, or wearing gaiters, or hunting, or something silly?

DOROTHY. No, Philip. It's that you're a very serious problem for any woman.

PHILIP. I hope so.

DOROTHY. And I don't want you to give up something. I want you to *take* up something.

PHILIP. Good.

[*He kisses her*]

I will. Now have some breakfast. I have to go back and make a few phone calls.

DOROTHY. Philip, don't go.

PHILIP. I'll be back in just a moment, darling. And I'll be *so* serious.

DOROTHY. You know what you said?

PHILIP. Of course.

DOROTHY. [*Very happily*] You said *Darling.*

PHILIP. I knew it was infectious but I never knew it was con-
tagious. Forgive me, *dear.*

DOROTHY. *Dear* is a nice word, too.

PHILIP. Good-bye then—er—sweet.

DOROTHY. Sweet, oh you *darling.*

PHILIP. Good-bye, Comrade.

DOROTHY. Comrade. Oh, and you said darling before.

PHILIP. Comrade's quite a word. I suppose I oughtn't to chuck
it around. I take it back.

DOROTHY. [*Rapturously*] Oh, Philip. *You're developing politically.*

PHILIP. God—er, oh you know, whatever it is, save us.

DOROTHY. Don't blaspheme. It's frightfully bad luck.

PHILIP. [*Hurriedly and rather grimly*] Good-bye, *darling dear
sweet.*

DOROTHY. You don't call me *comrade.*

PHILIP. [*Going out*] No. You see I'm developing politically.

[*He goes into the next room*]

DOROTHY. [*Rings for* PETRA. *Speaks to her. Leaning back com-
fortably in bed against the pillows*] Oh, Petra, he's so lovely and
so sort of *vital* and so gay. But he doesn't *do* anything. He's
supposed to send dispatches to some stupid London paper, but
they say at Censura he practically never sends anything. He's so
refreshing after Preston always going on about his wife and
children. Let him go *back* to his wife and children now if he's
so excited about them. I'll bet he won't. Those wife-and-children
men at a war. They just use them as sort of an opening wedge
to get into bed with some one and then immediately afterwards
they club you with them. I mean positively *club* you. I don't
know why I ever put up with Preston so long. And he's *so*
gloomy. Expecting the city to fall and everything and always
looking at the map. Always looking at a map is one of the most
irritating habits a man can get into. Isn't it, Petra?

PETRA. I don't understand, Señorita.

DOROTHY. Oh, Petra, I wonder what he's doing now.

PETRA. Nothing good.

DOROTHY. Petra, don't talk that way. You're a *defeatist*.

PETRA. No, Señorita, I have no politics. I only work.

DOROTHY. Well, you can go now because I think I'll go back to sleep for just a little while longer. I feel so sleepy and good this morning.

PETRA. That you rest well, Señorita.

> [*She goes out closing the door*]
> [*In the next room* PHILIP *answers the phone*]

PHILIP. Yes. Right. Send him up.

> [*There is a knock on the door and a* COMRADE *in I.B. uniform enters. He salutes smartly. He is a young, good-looking, dark boy of perhaps twenty-three*]

Salud, Comrade. Come in.

COMRADE. They sent me here from Brigade. I was to report to you in room one thirteen.

PHILIP. The room's changed. Do you have a copy of the order?

COMRADE. It was a verbal order.

> [PHILIP *takes the phone; asks for a number*]

PHILIP. *Ochenta—dos zero uno cinco.* Hello Haddock? No. Haddock. Hake speaking. Yes. Hake. Good. Haddock?

> [*He turns to the* COMRADE]

What's your name, Comrade?

COMRADE. Wilkinson.

PHILIP. Hello, Haddock. Sent a Comrade Wilkinson over to the Booth Fisheries? Right. Thanks so much. Salud.

> [*Hooks up the telephone. He turns to the* COMRADE *and puts out his hand*]

I'm glad to see you, Comrade. Now what was it?

COMRADE. I'm under your orders.

PHILIP. Oh.

> [*He seems very reluctant, about something*]

How old are you, Comrade?

COMRADE. Twenty.

PHILIP. Had much fun?

COMRADE. I'm not in this for fun.

PHILIP. No. Of course not. Was just a question.

[*He pauses. Then goes on abandoning the reluctance; he speaks in a very military way*]

Now one thing I have to tell you. In this particular show you have to be armed to enforce your authority. But you're not to use your weapon under any circumstances. Under any circumstances. Is that quite clear?

COMRADE. Not in self-defense?

PHILIP. Not under *any circumstances.*

COMRADE. I see. And what are my orders?

PHILIP. Go down and take yourself a walk. Then come back here and take a room and register. When you have the room stop by here and let me know what room it is, and I'll tell you what to do. You'll have to spend most of your time in your room today.

[*He pauses*]

Have a good walk. Might have a glass of beer. There's beer today at the Aguilar places.

COMRADE WILKINSON. I don't drink, Comrade.

PHILIP. Quite right. Excellent. We of the older generation have certain leprous spots of vice which can hardly be eradicated at this date. But you are an example to us. Get along now.

COMRADE WILKINSON. Yes, Comrade.

[*He salutes and goes out*]

PHILIP. [*After he has gone*] Awful pity. Yes. An awful pity.

[*The telephone rings*]

Yes? Here speaking. Good. No. I'm sorry. Later.

[*He hangs up the phone. . . . The phone rings again*]

Oh, hello. Yes. I'm awfully sorry. What a shame. I will. Yes. Later.

[*He hangs up. The phone rings again*]

Oh, hello. Oh, I am sorry, I really am. What do you say to a little later? No? Good man. Come in and we'll get it over with.

[*There is a knock at the door*]

Come on in.

[*Enter* PRESTON. *He has a bandaged eyebrow and looks none too well*]

I *am* sorry, you know.

PRESTON. What good does that do? You behaved disgustingly.

PHILIP. Right. Now what can I do?

[*Spoken very flatly*]

I said I was sorry.

PRESTON. Well, you might take off my dressing gown and slippers.

PHILIP. [*Taking them off*] Good.

[*He hands them over*]
[*Regretfully*]

You wouldn't sell the robe, would you? It's nice stuff.

PRESTON. No. And now get out of my room.

PHILIP. Do we have to do the whole thing over again?

PRESTON. If you won't get out I'll ring and have you thrown out.

PHILIP. Better ring, then.

[PRESTON *rings.* PHILIP *goes into the bathroom. There is a sound of water splashing. There is a knock at the door and the* MANAGER *enters*]

MANAGER. Nothing is all right?

PRESTON. I want you to call the police and have this man removed from my room.

MANAGER. Mr. Preston. I have maid pack your things up right away. You be comfortable in one fourteen. Mr. Preston you know better than call police into a hotel. What's a first thing police say? Whosa cana milk belong to? Whosa corn beef belong to? Whosa hoards coffee in this hotel? Whatsa meaning all this sugar in the armoire? Whosa got three bottles of whiskey? Whatsa matter here? Mr. Preston never calla police in private matter. Mr. Preston, I appeal to you.

PHILIP. [*From the bathroom*] Whosa these three cakesa soap belong to?

MANAGER. You see, Mr. Preston? In a private matter public authority is giva always a wrong interpretation. Is a law against to have these things. Is a severe law against all forms of hoarding. Is a police misunderstand.

PHILIP. [*From the bathroom*] Whosa got three bottles eau de cologne in here?

MANAGER. You see, Mr. Preston? With all my good voluntaries I could not introduce police.

PRESTON. Oh, go to—hell then, both of you. Have the things moved into one fourteen then. You're a rotten cad, Rawlings. Remember I told you, will you?

PHILIP. [*From the bathroom*] Whosa four tubes Mennen's shaving cream belong to?

MANAGER. Mister Preston. *Four* tubes. Mister Press-ton.

PRESTON. All you do is beg for food. I've given you plenty. Pack up the things and have them moved.

MANAGER. Very good, Mister Preston, but only one thing. When against all my voluntaries initiate slight petition for food only wishing superating quantities——

PHILIP. [*From bathroom, choking with laughing*] What's that?

MANAGER. Am telling Mr. Preston only petition unnecessary amounts and then only on basis of seven in family. Listen, Mr. Preston, has my mother-in-law—that luxury—now in her head one tooth remaining. You understand. Only one tooth. With this eats all and enjoys. When this goes must I buy entire apparatus of teeth both higher and lower, and is fit for eating higher things. Is fit for the *beef*steak, is fit for the chops, is fit for the what you call it, the *salomillo*. Every night I tell you, Mr. Preston, I ask her how is the tooth old woman? Every night I think if that goes where are *we*? Given entire new up and down teeth would not be enough horses left in Madrid for the army. I tell you, Mr. Preston, you never saw such a woman. Such a luxury. Mr. Preston, you unable spare one small can of any sort that superates?

PRESTON. Get something from Rawlings. He's your friend.

PHILIP. [*Coming out of the bathroom*] With me Comrade Stamp Collector superates one can of bully beef.

MANAGER. Oh, Mr. Philip. You have heart bigger than the hotel.

PRESTON. And twice as dirty.

[*He goes out*]

PHILIP. He's very bitter.

MANAGER. You take away the young lady. Makes him *furious*. Fills him with, how you call, jellishness.

PHILIP. That's it. He's simply crammed with jellishness. Tried to knock some of it out of him last night. No good.

MANAGER. Listen, Mr. Philip. Tell me one thing. How long the war going last?

PHILIP. A long time, I'm afraid.

MANAGER. Mr. Philip, I hate to hear you say *so*. Is now a year. Is not funny, you know.

PHILIP. Don't you worry about it. You just last yourself.

MANAGER. You be careful and last too. Mr. Philip, be more careful. I know. Don't think I don't know.

PHILIP. Don't know too much. And whatever you know keep your good old mouth shut, eh? We work all right together that way.

MANAGER. But be careful, Mr. Philip.

PHILIP. I'm lasting all right. Have a drink?

[*He pours a Scotch and puts water in it*]

MANAGER. Never I touch the alcohol. But listen, Mr. Philip. Be more careful. In one o five is very bad. In one o seven is very bad.

PHILIP. Thanks. I know that. Only what I had in one o seven I lost. They let him get away.

MANAGER. In one fourteen is only a fool.

PHILIP. Quite.

MANAGER. Last night is try get into one thirteen for you, pretending was mistake. I know.

PHILIP. That's why I wasn't there. I had some one looking after the fool.

MANAGER. Mr. Philip, you be very careful. You like I should put the Yale lock on door? The big lock? Very strongest type?

PHILIP. No. The big lock wouldn't do any good. You don't do this business with big locks.

MANAGER. You want anything special, Mr. Philip? Anything can do?

PHILIP. No. Nothing special. Thanks for turning away that fool journalist from Valencia who wanted a room here. We've got enough fools here now including you and me.

MANAGER. But I let him in later if you want. I told him was no room would let him know. If things quiet can let him in later on. Mr. Philip, you take care yourself. Please. You know.

PHILIP. I'm lasting well enough. I just get sort of low in my mind sometimes.

[*During this time* DOROTHY BRIDGES *has gotten out of bed, gone into the bathroom, dressed and come back to the room. She sits at the typewriter, then gets up and puts a record on the gramophone. It is a Chopin Ballade in La Bemol Menor Op. 47.* PHILIP *hears the music*]

PHILIP. [*To the* MANAGER] Excuse me a moment, will you? You going to move his things? If any one comes in for me ask them to wait, will you?

MANAGER. I tell the maid that moves.

[PHILIP *goes to* DOROTHY's *door and knocks*]

DOROTHY. Come in, Philip.
PHILIP. Mind if I have a drink in here for a moment?
DOROTHY. No. Please do.
PHILIP. Two things I'd like to ask you to do.

[*The record has stopped. In the other room you see that the* MANAGER *has gone out and that the* MAID *has come in and is making a pile of* PRESTON's *things on the bed*]

DOROTHY. What are they, Philip?
PHILIP. One is move out of this hotel, and the other is go back to America.
DOROTHY. Why, you impudent, impertinent man. Why you're worse than Preston.
PHILIP. I mean them both. This hotel's no place for you now. I mean it.

DOROTHY. And I was just beginning to be so happy with you. Philip, don't be silly. Please, darling, don't be silly.

[*At the door of the other room you see the* YOUNG COMRADE WILKINSON *in I.B. uniform at the open door*]

WILKINSON. [*To the* MAID] Comrade Rawlings?
MAID. Come in and sit down. He said to wait.

[WILKINSON *sits down in a chair with his back to the door. In the other room* DOROTHY *has put the record on the phonograph again.* PHILIP *lifts the needle off, and the record goes round and round on the turntable*]

DOROTHY. You said you wanted a drink. Here.
PHILIP. I don't want one.
DOROTHY. What's the matter, darling?
PHILIP. You know I'm being serious. You must get out of here.
DOROTHY. I'm not afraid of the shelling. You know that.
PHILIP. It's not the shelling.
DOROTHY. Well then, what is it, darling? Don't you like me? I'd like to make you very happy here.
PHILIP. What can I do to make you get out?
DOROTHY. Nothing. I won't go.
PHILIP. I'll have you moved over to the Victoria.
DOROTHY. You *will* not.
PHILIP. I wish I could talk to you.
DOROTHY. But why can't you?
PHILIP. I can't ever talk to any one.
DOROTHY. But darling, that's just an inhibition. You could go to an analyst and have that fixed in no time. It's easy and it's very fascinating.
PHILIP. You're hopeless. But you're beautiful. I'll just have you moved out.

[*He puts the needle back on the record and winds up the phonograph*]

PHILIP. I'm sorry if I seem dismal.
DOROTHY. It's probably just your liver, darling.

[*As the record plays, you see that some one has stopped outside the door of the room where the* MAID *is working*

*and the boy is sitting. The man is wearing a beret and a
trench coat, and he leans against the door jamb to steady
his aim and shoots the boy in the back of his head with a
long-barrelled Mauser pistol. The* MAID *screams—"Ayee"
—then starts to cry into her apron.* PHILIP, *as he hears the
shot, pushes* DOROTHY *toward the bed and goes to the door
with a pistol in his right hand. Opening the door he looks
both ways from it keeping himself covered, then rounds
the corner and enters the room. As the* MAID *sees him with
the pistol she screams again*]

PHILIP. Don't be silly.

*[He goes over to the chair where the body is, lifts the
head and lets it drop]*

The bastards. The dirty bastards.

*[*DOROTHY *had followed him to the door. He pushes her
out]*

PHILIP. Get out of here.
DOROTHY. Philip, what is it?
PHILIP. Don't look at him. That's a dead man. Somebody shot
him.
DOROTHY. Who shot him?
PHILIP. Maybe he shot himself. It's none of your business. Get
out of here. Didn't you ever see a dead man before? Aren't you
a lady war correspondent or something? Get out of here and
go and write an article. This is none of your business.

[Then to the MAID]

Hurry up and get those cans and bottles out of here.

*[He commences to throw things from the armoire shelves
onto the bed]*

All the cans of milk. *All* the corn beef. *All* the sugar. *All* the
tinned salmon. *All* the eau de cologne. *All* the extra soap. Get
them out. We have to call the police.

CURTAIN

END OF ACT I

ACT TWO · SCENE ONE

A room in Seguridad headquarters. There is a plain table, bare except for a green-shaded lamp. The windows are all closed and shuttered. Behind the table a short man with a very thin-lipped, hawk-nosed ascetic-looking face is sitting. He has very thick eyebrows. PHILIP *sits on a chair beside the table. The hawk-faced man is holding a pencil. On a chair in front of the table a* MAN *is sitting. He is crying with very deep shaking sobs.* ANTONIO (*the hawk-nosed man*) *is looking at him very interestedly. It is the* FIRST COMRADE *from Scene 3, Act 1. He is bareheaded, his tunic is off, and his braces, which hold up his baggy I.B. trousers, hang down along his trousers. As the curtain rises* PHILIP *stands up and looks at the* FIRST COMRADE.

PHILIP. [*In a tired voice*] I'd like to ask you one more thing.

FIRST COMRADE. Don't ask me. Please don't ask me. I don't want you to ask me.

PHILIP. Were you asleep?

FIRST COMRADE. [*Choking*] Yes.

PHILIP. [*In a very tired flat voice*] You know the penalty for that?

FIRST COMRADE. Yes.

PHILIP. Why didn't you say so at the start and save a lot of trouble? I wouldn't have you shot for that. I'm just disappointed in you now. Do you think people shoot people for fun?

FIRST COMRADE. I should have told you. I was frightened.

PHILIP. Yeah. You should have told me.

FIRST COMRADE. Truly, Comrade Commissar.

PHILIP. [*To* ANTONIO, *coldly*] You think he was asleep?

ANTONIO. How do I know? Do you want me to question him?

PHILIP. No, *mi Coronel*, no. We want information. We don't want a confession.

[*To the* FIRST COMRADE]

34

Listen, what did you dream about when you went to sleep?

FIRST COMRADE. [*Checks himself sobbing, hesitates, then goes on*] I don't remember.

PHILIP. Just try to. Take your time. I only want to be sure, you see. Don't try to lie. I'll know if you lie.

FIRST COMRADE. I remember now. I was against the wall and my rifle was between my legs when I leaned back, and I remember.

[*He chokes*]

In the dream I—I thought it was my girl and she was doing something—kind of funny—to me. I don't know what it was. It was just in a dream.

[*He chokes*]

PHILIP. [*To* ANTONIO] You satisfied now?

ANTONIO. I do not understand it completely.

PHILIP. Well, I guess nobody really understands it completely, but he's convinced me.

[*To the* FIRST COMRADE]

What's your girl's name?

FIRST COMRADE. Alma.

PHILIP. O.K. When you write her tell her she brought you a lot of luck.

[*To* ANTONIO]

As far as I'm concerned you can take him out. He reads the *Worker*. He knows Joe North. He's got a girl named Alma. He's got a good record with the Brigade, and he went to sleep and let a citizen slip who shot a boy named Wilkinson by mistake for me. The thing to do is to give him lots of strong coffee to keep him awake and keep rifles out from between his legs. Listen, Comrade, I'm sorry if I spoke roughly to you in the performance of my duty.

ANTONIO. I would like to put a few questions.

PHILIP. Listen, *mi Coronel*. If I wasn't good at this you wouldn't have let me go on doing it so long. This boy is all right. You know we are none of us *exactly* what you would call all *right*. But this boy is pretty all right. He just went to sleep, and I'm not justice, you know. I'm just working for you, and the cause, and the Republic and one thing and another. And we used to have a President named Lincoln in America, you know, who commuted sentences of sentries to be shot for sleeping, you know. So I think if it's all right with you we'll just sort of commute his sentence. He comes from the Lincoln Battalion you see—and it's an awfully good battalion. It's such a good battalion and it's done such things that it would break your damn heart if I tried to tell you about it. And if I was in it I'd feel decent and proud instead of the way I feel doing what I am. But I'm not, see? I'm a sort of a second-rate cop pretending to be a third-rate newspaper-man— But listen Comrade Alma——

[*Turning to prisoner*]

If you ever go to sleep again on duty when you are working for me I'll shoot you myself, see? You *hear* me? And write it to Alma.

ANTONIO. [*Ringing. Two* ASSAULT GUARDS *come in*] Take him away. You speak very confusedly, Philip. But you have a certain amount of credit to exhaust.

FIRST COMRADE. Thank you, Comrade Commissar.

PHILIP. Oh, don't say thank you in a war. This is a war. You don't say thank you in it. But you're welcome, see? And when you write to Alma tell her she brought you a lot of luck.

[FIRST COMRADE *goes out with* ASSAULT GUARDS]

ANTONIO. Yes, and now. This man got away from room 107 and shot this boy by mistake for you, and who is this man?

PHILIP. Oh, I don't know. Santa Claus, I guess. He's got a number. They have A numbered one to ten, and B numbered one to ten, and C numbered one to ten, and they shoot people and they blow up things and they do everything you're overly familiar with. And they work very hard, and aren't really awfully efficient. But they kill a lot of people that they shouldn't kill. The trouble is they've worked it out so well on the lines of the old Cuban A.B.C. that unless you get somebody outside that they deal with, it doesn't mean anything. It's just like cutting the heads off boils instead of listening to a Fleischman's Yeast Program. You know, correct me if I become confusing.

ANTONIO. And why do you not take this man with a sufficient force?

PHILIP. Because I cannot afford to make much noise and scare others that we need much more. This one is just a killer.

ANTONIO. Yes. There are plenty of fascists left in a town of a million people, and they work inside. Those who have the courage to. We must have twenty thousand active here.

PHILIP. More. Double that. But when you catch them they won't talk. Except the politicians.

ANTONIO. Politicians. Yes, politicians. I have seen a politician on the floor in that corner of the room unable to stand up when it was time to go out. I have seen a politician walk across that floor on his knees and put his arms around my legs and kiss my feet. I watched him slobber on my boots when all he had to do was such a simple thing as die. I have seen many die, and I have never seen a politician die well.

PHILIP. I don't like to see them die. It's O.K. I guess, if you like to see it. But I don't like it. Sometimes I don't know how you stick it. Listen, who dies well?

ANTONIO. You know. Don't be naïve.

PHILIP. Yes. I suppose I know.

ANTONIO. I could die all right. I don't ask any one to do something that is impossible.

PHILIP. You're a specialist. Look, Tonico. Who dies well? Go ahead, say it. Go ahead. Do you good to talk about your trade. Talk about it you know. Then next thing you know, forget it. Simple, eh? Tell me about in the first days of the movement.

ANTONIO. [*Rather proudly*] You want to hear? You mean definite people?

PHILIP. No. I know a couple of definite people. I mean sort of by classes.

ANTONIO. Fascists, real fascists, the young ones; very well. Sometimes with very much style. They are mistaken, but they have much style. Soldiers, yes, the majority all right. Priests all my life I am against. The church fights us. We fight the church. I am a Socialist for many years. We are the oldest revolutionary party in Spain. But to die——

[*He shakes his hand in the quick triple flip of the wrist that is the Spanish gesture of supreme admiration*]

To die? Priests? Terrific. You know; just simple priests. I don't
mean bishops.

PHILIP. And Antonio. Sometimes there must have been mistakes, eh? When you had to work in a hurry perhaps. Or you
know, just mistakes, we all make mistakes. I just made a little
one yesterday. Tell me, Antonio, were there ever any mistakes?

ANTONIO. Oh, yes. Certainly. Mistakes. Oh, yes. Mistakes. Yes.
Yes. Very regrettable mistakes. A very few.

PHILIP. And how did the mistakes die?

ANTONIO. [*Proudly*] All very well.

PHILIP. Ah——

> [*It is noise a boxer might make when he is hit with a
> hard body punch*]

And this trade we're in now. You know, what's the silly name
they call it? Counter-espionage. It doesn't ever get on your nerves?

ANTONIO. [*Simply*] No.

PHILIP. With me it's on the nerves now for a long time.

ANTONIO. But you've only been doing it for a little while.

PHILIP. Twelve bloody months, my boy, in this country. And
before that, Cuba. Ever been in Cuba?

ANTONIO. Yes.

PHILIP. That's where I got sucked in on all this.

ANTONIO. How were you sucked in?

PHILIP. Oh, people started trusting me that should have known
better. And I suppose because they should have known better I
started getting, you know, sort of trustworthy. You know, not
elaborately, just sort of moderately trustworthy. And then they
trust you a little more and you do it all right. And then you
know, you get to believing in it. Finally I guess you get to liking
it. I have a sort of a feeling I don't explain it very well.

ANTONIO. You're a good boy. You work well. Everybody trusts
you very much.

PHILIP. Too bloody much. And I'm tired too, and I'm worried
right now. You know what I'd like? I'd like to never kill another
son-of-a-bitch, I don't care who or for what, as long as I live.
I'd like to never have to lie. I'd like to know who I'm with when
I wake up. I'd like to wake up in the same place every morning
for a week straight. I'd like to marry a girl named Bridges that

you don't know. But don't mind if I use the name because I like to say it. And I'd like to marry her because she's got the longest, smoothest, straightest legs in the world, and I don't have to listen to her when she talks if it doesn't make too good sense. But I'd like to see what the kids would look like.

ANTONIO. She is the tall blonde with that correspondent?

PHILIP. Don't talk about her like that. She isn't any tall blonde with some correspondent. That's my girl. And if I talk too much or take up your valuable time, why, stop me. You know I'm a very extraordinary fellow. I can talk either English or American. Was brought up in one, raised in the other. That's what I make my living at.

ANTONIO. [Soothingly] I know. You are tired, Philip.

PHILIP. Well, now I'm talking American. Bridges is the same way. Only I'm not sure she can talk American. You see she learned her English at college and from the cheap or literary type of Lord, but you know what's funny, you see. I just like to hear her talk. I don't care what she says. I'm relaxed now, you see. I haven't had anything to drink since breakfast, and I'm a lot drunker than I am when I drink, and that's a bad sign. Is it all right for one of your operatives to relax, mi Coronel?

ANTONIO. You ought to go to bed. You're tired out, Philip, and you have much work to do.

PHILIP. That's right. I'm tired out and I have much work to do. I'm waiting to meet a comrade at Chicote's. Name of Max. I have, and I do not exaggerate, very much work to do. Max, whom I believe you know and who, to show what a distinguished man he is, has no hind name, while my back name is Rawlings exactly the same as when I started. Which shows you I haven't gotten very far in this business. What was I saying?

ANTONIO. About Max.

PHILIP. Max. That's it. Max. Well he's a day overdue now. He's been navigating now for about two weeks, say circulating to avoid confusion, behind the fascist lines. It's his specialty. And he says, and he doesn't lie. I lie. But not right now. Anyway, I'm very tired, see, and I'm also disgusted with my job, and I'm nervous as a bastard because I'm worried and I don't worry easy.

ANTONIO. Go on. Don't be temperamental.

PHILIP. He says, that is Max says, and where he is now I wish to hell I knew, that he has a place located, an observation post, you know. Watch them fall, and say it's the wrong place. One of those. Well, he says that the German head of the siege artillery that shells this town comes there and a lovely politician. You know a museum piece. He comes there too. And *Max* thinks. And *I* think he is screwball. But he thinks better. I think *faster*, but he thinks better. That we can bag those citizens. Now listen very carefully, *mi Coronel*, and correct me instantly. I think it sounds very romantic. But *Max* says, and he's a German and very practical, and he'd just as soon go behind the fascist lines as you would go to get a shave, or what shall we say. Well *he* says it's perfectly practical. So *I* thought. And I'm sort of drunk now on drinking nothing for so long. That we would sort of suspend the other projects that we have been working on, temporarily, and try to get these two people for you. I don't think the German is of much practical use to you, but he has a very high exchange value indeed, and this project sort of, in a way, appeals to Max. Lay it to nationalism, I say. But if we get this other citizen you've got something, *mi Coronel*. Because he is very, *very* terrific. I mean *terrific*. He, you see, is *outside* the town. But he knows who is *inside* the town. And then you just sort of bring him into good voice and *you* know who is inside the town. Because they all communicate with him. I talk too much, don't I?

ANTONIO. Philip.

PHILIP. Yes, Mi Coronel.

ANTONIO. Philip, now go to Chicote's and get drunk like a good boy and do your work, and come or call when you have news.

PHILIP. And what do I talk, *mi Coronel*, American or English?

ANTONIO. What you like. Do not talk silly. But go now, please, because we are good friends and I like you very much, but I am very busy. Listen, is it true about the observation post?

PHILIP. Yeah.

ANTONIO. What a thing.

PHILIP. Very fancy, though. Awfully, *awfully* fancy, *mi Coronel*.

ANTONIO. Go, please, and start.

PHILIP. And I talk either English or American?

ANTONIO. What's all that about? Go.

PHILIP. Then I'll talk English. Christ, I can lie so much easier in English, it's pitiful.

ANTONIO. GO. GO. GO. GO. GO.

PHILIP. Yes, *mi Coronel*. Thank you for the instructive little talk. I'll go to Chicote's now. *Salud, mi Coronel*.

[*He salutes, looks at his watch and goes*]

ANTONIO. [*At the desk, looks after him. Then rings. Two* ASSAULT GUARDS *come in. They salute*] Now just bring me in that man you took out before. I want to talk to him a little while alone by myself.

CURTAIN

ACT TWO · SCENE TWO

A corner table at Chicote's bar. It is the first table on your right as you enter the door. The door and the window are sandbagged about three quarters of the way up. PHILIP *is seated at the table with* ANITA. *A* WAITER *comes over to the table.*

PHILIP. Any of the barrel whiskey left?

WAITER. Nothing now of the real but gin.

PHILIP. Good gin?

WAITER. The yellow of Booth's. The best.

PHILIP. With bitters.

ANITA. You don't love any more?

PHILIP. No.

ANITA. You make big mistake with that big blonde.

PHILIP. What *big* blonde?

ANITA. That great big blonde. Tall like a tower. Big like a horse.

PHILIP. Blonde like a wheat field.

ANITA. You make a mistake. Big a woman. Big a mistake.

PHILIP. What makes you think she's so big?

ANITA. Big? Is big like a tank. Wait you get her with a baby. Big? Is a Studebaker truck.

PHILIP. That's a lovely word, Studebaker, as you say it.

ANITA. Yes. I like best any English word I know. Studebaker. Is beautiful. Why you no love?

PHILIP. I don't know, Anita. You know. Things change.

[*He looks at his watch*]

ANITA. You use a like fine. Is just the same.

PHILIP. I know it.

ANITA. You like before. You like again. Is must only try.

PHILIP. I know.

ANITA. When is have something good you don't want to go away. Is a big woman plenty trouble. I know. I been this a long time.

PHILIP. You're a fine girl, Anita.

ANITA. Is on account they all criticize because I bite Mr. Vernon that time?

PHILIP. No. Of course not.

ANITA. I tell you I give a lot not to do that.

PHILIP. Oh, nobody remembers that.

ANITA. You know why I do? Everybody know I bite, but nobody ever ask why.

PHILIP. Why was it?

ANITA. He try to take three hundred pesetas out my stocking. What I should do? Say "Yes, go ahead. All right. Help yourself"? No, I bite.

PHILIP. Quite right, too.

ANITA. You think? Really?

PHILIP. Yes.

ANITA. Oh, you sweet all right. Listen, you don't want make mistake now with that big blonde.

PHILIP. You know, Anita. I'm afraid I do. I'm afraid that's the whole trouble. I want to make an absolutely colossal mistake.

[*He calls the* WAITER, *looks at his watch. To* WAITER]

What time have you?

WAITER. [*Looks at the clock over the bar and at Philip's watch*] The same as you have.

ANITA. Be colossal all right.

PHILIP. You're not jealous?

ANITA. No. I just hate. Last night I try to like. I say hokay everybody a comrade. Comes a big bombardment. Maybe everybody killed. Should be comrades everybody with each other. Bury the axes. Not be selfish. Not be egotistic. Love a enemy like a self. All that slop.

PHILIP. You were terrific.

ANITA. That kind a stuff don't last over the night. This morning I wake up. First thing I do I hate that woman all day long.

PHILIP. You mustn't, you know.

ANITA. What she want with you? She take a man just like you pick a flowers. She don't want. She just pick to put in her room. She just like you because you big, too. Listen. I like you if you was a dwarf.

PHILIP. Na, Anita. No. Be careful.

ANITA. Listen good. I like you if you was sick. I like you if dry up and be ugly. I like you if you hunchback.

PHILIP. Hunchbacks are lucky.

ANITA. I like you if you *unlucky* hunchback. I like you if you got no money. You want? I make it.

PHILIP. That's about the only thing I haven't tried on this job.

ANITA. I not joke. I'm a serious. Philip, you leave her alone. You come back where you know is hokay.

PHILIP. I'm afraid I can't, Anita.

ANITA. You just try. Isn't any change. You like before, you like again. Always works that way when a man is a man.

PHILIP. But you see I change. It's not that I mean to.

ANITA. You no change. I know you good. I know you long time now. You not the kind that change.

PHILIP. All men change.

ANITA. Is not the truth. Is get tired, yes. Is want to go away, yes. Is run around, yes. Is get angry, yes, yes. Is treat bad, yes, plenty. Is change? No. Only is to start different habits. Is a habit is all. Right away is the same with whoever.

PHILIP. I see that. Yes, that's right. But you see it's this sort of running into some one from your own people, and it upsets you.

ANITA. Is not from your own people. Is not like you. Is a different breed of people.

PHILIP. No, it's the same sort of people.

ANITA. Listen, that big blonde make you crazy already. This soon you can't think good. Is no more the same as you as blood

and paint. Is look the same. Can a blood Can a paint. All right.
Put the paint in the body, instead of blood. What you get?
American woman.

PHILIP. You're unjust to her, Anita. Granted she's lazy and
spoiled, and rather stupid, and enormously on the make. Still
she's very beautiful, very friendly, and very charming and rather
innocent—and quite brave.

ANITA. Hokay. Beautiful? What you want with beautiful when
you're through? I know you. Friendly? Hokay; is friendly can be
unfriendly. Charming? Yes. Is a charming like the snake with
rabbits. Innocent? You make me laugh. Ha, ha, ha. Is a innocent
until a prove the guilty. Brave? Brave? You make me laugh again
if I have any laugh left in my belly. Brave? All right. I laugh.
Ho, ho, ho. What you do all the time this war you can't tell a
ignorance from a brave? Brave? My this——

[*She rises from the table and slaps her behind*]

So. Now I go.

PHILIP. You're awfully hard on her.

ANITA. Hard on her? I like to throw a hand grenade in the bed
where she sleeping right this minute. I tell you true. Last night
I try all that stuff. All that sacrifice. All that giveup. You know.
Now have one good *healthy* feeling. I hate.

[*She goes*]

PHILIP. [*To the* WAITER] You haven't seen a comrade from
the International Brigades here asking for me? Name of Max? A
comrade with a face sort of broken across here.

[*He puts his hand across his mouth and jaw*]

A comrade with his teeth gone in front? With sort of black
gums where they burnt them with a red-hot iron? And with a
scar here?

[*He runs his finger across the lower angle of his jaw*]

Have you seen such a comrade?

WAITER. He hasn't been here.

PHILIP. If such a comrade comes, will you ask him to come to
the hotel?

WAITER. What hotel?

PHILIP. He'll know what hotel.

[*Starts out and looks back*]

Tell him I went out looking for him.

CURTAIN

ACT TWO · SCENE THREE

Same as Act I Scene III. The two adjoining rooms 109 and 110 in the Hotel Florida. It is dark outside the rooms and the curtains are drawn. There is no one in room 110 and it is dark. Room 109 is lighted brightly both by the reading lamp on the table, the main light in the ceiling, and a reading lamp clamped to the head of the bed. The electric heater and the electric stove are both on. DOROTHY BRIDGES, *wearing a turtle-neck sweater, a tweed skirt, wool stockings and jodhpur boots, is doing something with a long-handled stew-pan on the electric cooking ring. A distant noise of gun fire comes through the curtained windows.* DOROTHY *rings the bell. There is no answering sound. She rings again.*

DOROTHY. Oh, damn that electrician!

[*She goes to the door and opens it*]

Petra! Oh, Petra!

[*You hear the* MAID *coming down the hall. She comes in the door*]

PETRA. Yes, Señorita?

DOROTHY. Where's the electrician, Petra?

PETRA. Didn't you know?

DOROTHY. No. What? He's simply got to come and fix this bell!

PETRA. He can't come, Señorita, because he's dead.

DOROTHY. What do you say?

PETRA. He was hit last night when he went out during the bombardment.

DOROTHY. He went out during the bombardment?

PETRA. Yes, Señorita. He had been drinking a little, and he went out to go home.

DOROTHY. The poor little man!

PETRA. Yes, Señorita, it was a shame!

DOROTHY. How was he hit, Petra?

PETRA. Some one shot him from a window, they say. I don't know. That's what they told me.

DOROTHY. Who'd shoot him from a window?

PETRA. Oh, they always shoot from windows at night during a bombardment. The fifth column people. The people who fight us from inside the city.

DOROTHY. But why would they shoot him? He was only a poor little workman.

PETRA. They could see he was a workingman from his clothes.

DOROTHY. Of course, Petra.

PETRA. That's why they shot him. They are our enemies. Even of me. If I was killed they would be happy. They would think it was one working person less.

DOROTHY. But it's *dreadful!*

PETRA. Yes, Señorita.

DOROTHY. But it's terrible. You mean they shoot at people that they don't even know who they are?

PETRA. Oh, yes. They are our enemies.

DOROTHY. They're terrible people!

PETRA. Yes, Señorita!

DOROTHY. And what will we do for an *electricista?*

PETRA. Tomorrow we can get another. But now they would all be closed. You should not burn so many lights perhaps, Señorita, and then perhaps the fuse will not melt out. Use only what you need to see.

[DOROTHY *turns off all but the reading light on the bed*]

DOROTHY. Now I can't even see to cook this mess. I suppose that's better though. It didn't say on the tin whether you could heat it or not. It will probably be frightful!

PETRA. What are you cooking, Señorita?

DOROTHY. I don't know, Petra. There wasn't any label on it.

PETRA. [*Peering into the pot*] It looks like rabbit.

DOROTHY. What looks like rabbit is cat. But I don't think they'd bother to put cat up in a tin and ship it all the way from Paris, do you? Of course, they may have tinned it in Barcelona and then shipped it to Paris and then flown it down here. Do you think it's cat, Petra?

PETRA. If it's put up in Barcelona, you can't tell what it is!

DOROTHY. Oh, I'm sick of the whole thing. You go ahead and cook it, Petra!

PETRA. Yes, Señorita. What should I put in?

DOROTHY. [*Picking up a book and going over to the reading light to stretch out on the bed*] Put in anything. Open a tin of anything.

PETRA. Is it for Mr. Philip?

DOROTHY. If he comes.

PETRA. Mr. Philip wouldn't like just anything. It would be better to put in carefully for Mr. Philip. One time he threw a whole breakfast tray on the floor.

DOROTHY. Why, Petra?

PETRA. It was something he read in the paper.

DOROTHY. It was Eden, probably. He hates Eden.

PETRA. Still it was a very violent thing to do. I told him he had no right. *No hay derecho,* I told him.

DOROTHY. And what did he do?

PETRA. He helped me pick it all up, and then he slapped me here when I was bending over. Señorita, I do not like to see him in that next room. He is a different cultural than you.

DOROTHY. I love him, Petra.

PETRA. Señorita! Please do not do such a thing. You haven't done his room and made his bed for seven months as I have. Señorita, he's *bad*. I do not say he is not a good man. But he is *bad*.

DOROTHY. You mean he's wicked?

PETRA. No. Not wicked. Wicked is dirty. He is very clean. He takes baths all the time even with cold water. Even in the coldest weather he washes his feet. But, Señorita, he is not good. And he will not make you happy.

DOROTHY. But Petra, he made me happier than any one has ever made me.

PETRA. Señorita, that is nothing.

DOROTHY. What do you mean, that's *nothing?*

PETRA. Here everybody can do that!

DOROTHY. You're just a nation of braggarts. Do I have to listen to all that about *conquistadores* and all that?

PETRA. I only meant that is a badness here. A good man has that too, perhaps, yes, a really good man such as I was married to has that. But *all* bad men have that.

DOROTHY. You mean to hear them talk they have it.

PETRA. No. Señorita.

DOROTHY. [*Intrigued*] You mean they really . . . ?

PETRA. [*Sadly*] Yes, Señorita.

DOROTHY. I don't believe a word of it. And you think Mr. Philip is a *really* bad man?

PETRA. [*Earnestly*] Frightful!

DOROTHY. Oh, I *wonder* where he is?

> [*There is a noise of heavy boots coming down the corridor.* PHILIP *and* THREE COMRADES *in I.B. uniform enter 110, and* PHILIP *switches on the light.* PHILIP *is bare-headed, wet, and dishevelled looking. One of the* COMRADES *is* MAX, *the one with the broken face. He is covered with mud and as they come into the room, he sits down on a chair before the table, facing the back of the chair, and resting his hands and his chin on the top of the back of the chair. He has an amazing face. One of the other* COMRADES *has a short automatic rifle slung over his shoulder. The other has a long Mauser parabellum pistol in a wooden holster strapped to his leg.*]

PHILIP. I want you to block these two rooms off the corridor. Any one to see me *you* bring them in. How many comrades have you below?

The COMRADE *with the rifle.* Twenty-five.

PHILIP. Here are the keys to room one o eight and one eleven.

> [*He hands one to each*]

Have the doors open and stand just inside the door, so you can watch the corridor. No, better get a chair apiece and sit inside the door where you can watch. All right. Get along. . . . Comrades!

> [THEY *salute and go out.* PHILIP *goes over to the broken-faced* COMRADE. *He puts his hand on his shoulder. The audience has seen for several moments that he is asleep, but* PHILIP *does not know it*]

PHILIP. Max.

> [MAX *wakes, looks at* PHILIP *and smiles*]

Was it very bad, Max?

> [MAX *looks at him and smiles again and shakes his head*]

MAX. *Nicht zu schwer.*
PHILIP. And when comes he?
MAX. In the evenings of grand bombardment.
PHILIP. And where?
MAX. To the roof of a house at the top of Extremadura road. It has a little tower.
PHILIP. I thought he came to Garabitas.
MAX. So did I.
PHILIP. And when gives more grand bombardment?
MAX. Tonight.
PHILIP. When?
MAX. *Fiertel nach zwölf.*
PHILIP. You're sure?
MAX. You should see the shells. Everything all laid out. Also they are very sloppy soldiers. If I did not have this face I could have stayed and worked a gun. Maybe they put me on the staff even.
PHILIP. Where did you change the uniform? I was out there looking for you at a couple of places.
MAX. In one of the houses in Carabanchel. There are a hundred to pick from in that stretch that no one holds. A hundred and four, I think. Between our lines and theirs. Over there it was all right. The soldiers are all young. It was only if an officer should see my face. An officer would know where these faces come from.
PHILIP. So now?
MAX. I think we go tonight. Why wait?

PHILIP. How is it?

MAX. Muddy.

PHILIP. How many do you need?

MAX. You and me. Or whoever you send with me.

PHILIP. Me.

MAX. Good! Now how is it to take a bath?

PHILIP. Fine! Go ahead.

MAX. And I sleep a little while.

PHILIP. What time should we leave?

MAX. By half past nine.

PHILIP. Get some sleep then.

MAX. You call me?

[*He goes into the bathroom.* PHILIP *goes out of the room, closes the door, and knocks on the door of 109*]

DOROTHY. [*From the bed*] Come in!

PHILIP. Hello, darling.

DOROTHY. Hello.

PHILIP. Are you cooking?

DOROTHY. I was, but I got bored with it. Are you hungry?

PHILIP. Famished.

DOROTHY. It's in the pot there. Turn on the stove and it will warm up.

PHILIP. What's the matter with you, Bridges?

DOROTHY. Where have you been?

PHILIP. Just out in the town.

DOROTHY. Doing what?

PHILIP. Just around.

DOROTHY. You've left me alone all day. Ever since that poor man was shot in there this morning you've left me alone. I've waited in here the whole day. No one's even been to see me all day except Preston and he was so unpleasant I had to ask him to leave. Where have you been?

PHILIP. Just around and about.

DOROTHY. Chicote's?

PHILIP. Yes.

DOROTHY. And did you see that horrible Moor?

PHILIP. Oh, yes, Anita. She sent messages.

DOROTHY. She's unspeakable! You can keep the messages.

[PHILIP *has ladled some of the contents of the stew-pan onto a plate and tastes it*]

PHILIP. I say. What is this?

DOROTHY. I don't know.

PHILIP. I say. It's jolly good. Did you cook it yourself?

DOROTHY. [*Coyly*] Yes. Do you like it?

PHILIP. I didn't know you could cook.

DOROTHY. [*Shyly*] Really, Philip?

PHILIP. I say it *is* good! But what gave you the idea of putting kippers in it?

DOROTHY. Oh, damn Petra! So that was the other tin she opened.

[*There is a knock on the door. It is the* MANAGER. *One of his arms is firmly held by the* COMRADE *with the automatic rifle*]

RIFLE COMRADE. This comrade here said he wanted to see you.

PHILIP. Thank you, Comrade. Let him come in.

[*The* RIFLE COMRADE *turns the* MANAGER *loose and salutes*]

MANAGER. It was an absolutely nothing, Mr. Philip. Passing in hall with overkeenness of smell produced by hunger, detected odor of cooking and stopped. Instantly was seized by the comrade. Perfectly all right, Mr. Philip. Absolutely nothing. Do not concern yourself. *Buen provecho,* Mr. Philip. Eat well, Madame.

PHILIP. You came by just at the right moment. I have something for you. Take this.

[*Hands him the casserole, the plate, the fork, and ladle, with both hands*]

MANAGER. Mr. Philip. No. I cannot.

PHILIP. Comrade Stamp Collector, you must!

MANAGER. No, Mr. Philip.

[*Taking them*]

I cannot. You move me to the tears. I could never. It is too much!

PHILIP. Comrade, not a word more!

MANAGER. You dissolve my heart in feeling. Mr. Philip, from my heart his bottom, I thank you.

[*He goes out, holding the plate in one hand, the stew-pan in the other.*]

DOROTHY. Philip, I'm sorry.

PHILIP. If you don't mind, I'll take a little whiskey with plain water. Then you might open a tin of the bully beef and slice up an onion.

DOROTHY. But Philip, darling, I can't bear the smell of onions!

PHILIP. Chances are that won't bother us tonight.

DOROTHY. You mean you're not going to be here?

PHILIP. I have to go out.

DOROTHY. Why?

PHILIP. With the boys.

DOROTHY. I know what that means.

PHILIP. Do you?

DOROTHY. Yes. Only too well.

PHILIP. Ghastly, isn't it?

DOROTHY. It's hateful! The whole way you waste your time and your life is hateful and stupid.

PHILIP. And me so young and promising.

DOROTHY. You're nasty to go out tonight when we could stay and have a lovely evening like last night.

PHILIP. It's the beast in me.

DOROTHY. But Philip, you could stay here. You can drink right here or do anything you want. I'll be gay and play the phonograph. I'll drink too, even if it gives me a headache afterwards. We'll get a lot of people in if you want a lot of people. It can be noisy and full of smoke, and everything you like. You don't have to go out, Philip!

PHILIP. Come here and kiss me!

[*He holds her in his arms*]

DOROTHY. And don't eat onions, Philip. If you don't eat the onions, I'll feel surer of you.

PHILIP. All right. I won't eat the onions. Have you any tomato catsup?

[*There is a knock at the door. It is the* RIFLE COMRADE *again with the* MANAGER]

RIFLE COMRADE. This comrade back here again!

PHILIP. Thank you, Comrade. Let him in.

[RIFLE COMRADE *salutes and goes out*]

MANAGER. Is just come tell you all right can take a joke, Mr. Philip. Is a sense of humor O.K.

[*Sadly*]

Is a food right now not to joke with. Neither is to spoil, maybe, if you think it over. But is all right. I take the joke.

PHILIP. Take a couple of tins of this.

[*He gives him two tins of corned beef from the armoire*]

DOROTHY. Whose beef is that?

PHILIP. Oh, I suppose it's your beef.

MANAGER. Thank you, Mr. Philip. Is a good joke all right. Ha, ha. Expensive all right, yes, maybe. But thank you, Mr. Philip. Thank *you*, too, Miss.

[*He goes out*]

PHILIP. Look, Bridges.

[*He puts his arms around her*]

Don't mind me if I'm stuffy tonight.

DOROTHY. Darling, all I want is for you to stay in. I want us to have some sort of home-life. It's nice here. I could fix up your room and make it attractive.

PHILIP. It got a touch messy this morning.

DOROTHY. I'd fix it up so you'd like it to live in. You could have a comfortable chair and a bookcase, and a good reading light, and pictures. I could fix it really nicely. Please stay here tonight and just see how nice it is.

PHILIP. Tomorrow night.

DOROTHY. Why not tonight, darling?

PHILIP. Oh, tonight's one of those restless nights when you feel you have to get out and buzz around and see people. And, besides, I have an appointment.

DOROTHY. At what time?

PHILIP At a quarter past twelve.

DOROTHY. Then come back afterwards.

PHILIP. All right.

DOROTHY. Come in any time.

PHILIP. Really——?

DOROTHY. Yes. Please.

[*He takes her in his arms. He strokes her hair. Tips her head back and kisses her. There is noise of shouting and singing downstairs. Then you hear the* COMRADES *break into "The Partizan." They sing it all the way through*]

DOROTHY. That's a lovely song.

PHILIP. You'll never know how fine a song that is.

[*The* COMRADES *are singing "Bandera Rosa"*]

PHILIP. You know this one?

[*He sits by her now on the bed*]

DOROTHY. Yes.

PHILIP. The best people I ever knew died for that song.

[*In the next room you can see the broken-faced* COMRADE *asleep. While they have been talking, he finished his bath, dried his clothes, knocked the mud off them, and lay down on the bed. As he sleeps, the light shines on his face*]

DOROTHY. [*Beside Philip, on the bed*] Philip, Philip, please, Philip!

PHILIP. You know I don't feel so much like making love tonight.

DOROTHY. [*Disappointed*] That's fine. That's lovely! But I'd only like to have you stay here. Just stay in and have a little home-life.

PHILIP. I have to go, you know. Really.

[*Downstairs the* COMRADES *are singing the "Comintern" song*]

DOROTHY. That's the one they always play at funerals.

PHILIP. They sing it at other times, though.

DOROTHY. Philip, please don't go!

PHILIP. [*Holding her in his arms*] Good-bye.

DOROTHY. No. Please, please, don't go!

PHILIP. [*Standing up*] Look, open both the windows before you go to bed, will you? You don't want to have any glass broken if there's a shelling around midnight.

DOROTHY. Don't go, Philip. Please don't go!

PHILIP. Salud, Camarada!

> [*He does not salute. He goes into the next room. Downstairs the* COMRADES *are singing the "Partizan" again.* PHILIP, *in 110, looks at* MAX *sleeping; then goes over to wake him*]

Max!

> [MAX, *waking instantly, looks around him, blinks at the light in his eyes, then smiles*]

MAX. Is time?

PHILIP. Yes. Want a drink?

MAX. [*Getting up from the bed, smiling, and feeling of his boots, which have been drying in front of the electric heater*] Very much.

> [PHILIP *pours two whiskeys and reaches for the water bottle*]

Do not spoil it with water.

PHILIP. Salud!

MAX. Salud!

PHILIP. Let's go.

CURTAIN

> [*Downstairs the* COMRADES *are singing the "International." As the curtain comes down,* DOROTHY BRIDGES *is on the bed in Room 109, with her arms around the pillows; and her shoulders shaking as she is crying*]

ACT TWO · SCENE FOUR

Same as Scene III, but four thirty o'clock in the morning. Both rooms are dark and DOROTHY BRIDGES *is asleep in her bed.* MAX *and* PHILIP *come down the corridor, and* PHILIP

*unlocks the door of Room 110 and switches on the light.
They look at each other. MAX shakes his head. They are
both so covered with mud that they are almost unrecog-
nizable.*

PHILIP. Well, another time.

MAX. I am very sorry.

PHILIP. It's not your fault. Want to bathe first?

MAX. [*His head on his arms*] Go ahead and take it. I am too
tired.

[PHILIP *goes into the bathroom. Then comes out*]

PHILIP. There's no hot water. Only reason we live in this damn
death trap is for hot water, and now there's none!

MAX. [*Very sleepily*] I am very sad to fail. I was certain they
were coming. But they did not come.

PHILIP. Get your clothes off, and get some sleep. You're a
marvellous bloody damned scout officer, and you know it. Nobody could do what you've done . . . it's not your fault if they
call off the shoot.

MAX. [*Really utterly and completely exhausted*] I am too
sleepy. I am so sleepy I am sick.

PHILIP. Come on, I'll get you to bed.

[*He pulls his boots off and helps him to undress.* PHILIP
tumbles him into bed]

MAX. The bed is good.

[*He takes hold of the pillow with his arms and spreads
his legs wide*]

I sleep on my face, and then it does not frighten anybody in the
morning.

PHILIP. [*From the bathroom*] Take the whole bed. I'm bunking
in another room.

[PHILIP *goes into the bathroom and you hear him splashing. He comes out in pajamas and a dressing gown, opens
the door connecting the two rooms, ducks under the poster
and goes over to the bed and climbs in*]

DOROTHY. [*In the dark*] Darling, is it late?

PHILIP. Fiveish.

DOROTHY. [*Very sleepily*] Where have you been?

PHILIP. On a visit.

DOROTHY. [*Who is still really asleep*] Did you keep your appointment?

PHILIP. [*Rolling away to one side of the bed so that he is back to back with her*] The man didn't show up.

DOROTHY. [*Very sleepily, but anxious to impart news*] There wasn't any shelling, darling.

PHILIP. Good!

DOROTHY. Good night, darling.

PHILIP. Good night!

[*You hear a machine-gun go pop-pop-pop a long way away through the open window. They lie very quietly in the bed and then we hear* PHILIP *say*]

Bridges, are you asleep?

DOROTHY. [*Really asleep*] No, darling. Not if——

PHILIP. I want to tell you something.

DOROTHY. [*Sleepily*] Yes, my very dear.

PHILIP. I want to tell you two things. I've got the horrors, and I love you.

DOROTHY. Oh, you poor Philip.

PHILIP. I never tell anybody when I get the horrors, and I never tell anybody I love them. But I love you, see? Do you hear me? Do you feel me? Do you hear me say it?

DOROTHY. Why, I love you all the time. And you feel lovely. Sort of like a snow storm if snow wasn't cold and didn't melt.

PHILIP. I don't love you in the daytime. I don't love anything in the daytime. Listen, I want to say something else. Would you like to marry me or stay with me all the time or go wherever I go, and be my girl? Hear me say it? I said it, see.

DOROTHY. Darling, I'd like to *marry* you.

PHILIP. Yeah. I say funny things in the night, don't I?

DOROTHY. I'd like us to be married and work hard and have a fine life. You know I'm not as silly as I sound, or I wouldn't be here. And I work when you're not around. And just because I can't cook. You can hire people to cook under normal circumstances. Oh, you. I love you with the big shoulders and the walk like a gorilla and the funny face.

PHILIP. It'll be a lot funnier face when I get through with this business.

DOROTHY. Are the horrors any better, darling? Do you want to tell me about them?

PHILIP. Oh, the hell with them. I've had them so long I'd miss them if they went away. Let me say one thing more to you.

[*He says it very slowly*]

I'd like to marry you, and go away, and get out of all this. Did I say it just like that? Did you hear me say it?

DOROTHY. Well, darling, we will.

PHILIP. No, we won't. Even lying in the night I know we won't. But I like to say it. Oh, I love you. Goddamn it, goddamn it, I love you. And you've got the loveliest damn body in the world. And I adore you, too. Did you hear me say that?

DOROTHY. Yes, my sweet, but it's not true about my body. It's just an all right body, but I like to hear you say it. And tell me about the horrors, and maybe they will go away.

PHILIP. No. Everybody gets their own, and you don't want to pass them around.

DOROTHY. Should we try to go to sleep, my big lovely one? My old snow storm.

PHILIP. It's getting almost daylight, and I'm getting sensible again.

DOROTHY. Please try to go to sleep.

PHILIP. Listen, Bridges, while I say something else. It's getting light now.

DOROTHY. [*Her voice catching*] Yes, darling.

PHILIP. If you want me to go to sleep, Bridges, just hit me on the head with a hammer.

CURTAIN

END OF ACT TWO

ACT THREE · SCENE ONE

*TIME: Five days later. It is afternoon in the same two
rooms in the Hotel Florida, 109 and 110.*

*The scene is the same as Scene III Act II except that the
door is open between the two rooms. The poster flaps
open at the bottom in* PHILIP's *room, on the night
table by the bed, there is a vase full of chrysanthemums.
There is a bookcase along the wall to the right of the bed,
and cretonne covers on the chairs. There are curtains on
the windows, of the same cretonne, and the bed has a
cover over its white spread. All clothes are hung neatly on
hangers, and three pairs of* PHILIP's *boots, all brushed and
polished, are being put into the closet by* PETRA. DOROTHY
*in the next room, 109, is trying on a silver fox cape before
the mirror.*

DOROTHY. Petra, please come here!
PETRA. [*Straightening her little and old body up from putting
the boots away*] Yes, Señorita!

[PETRA *goes around and comes in by the proper door to
109, knocking as she opens it*]

PETRA. [*Holding her hands together*] Oh, Señorita, it's beautiful!
DOROTHY. [*Looking over her shoulder into the mirror*] It's not
right, Petra. I don't know *what* they've done, but it's *not* right!
PETRA. It looks lovely, Señorita!
DOROTHY. No, there's something wrong with the top of the
collar. And I can't speak Spanish well enough to explain to that
fool of a furrier. He *is* a fool.

[*You hear some one coming down the hall. It is* PHILIP.
*He opens the door to 110 and looks around. He takes off
his leather coat, and tosses it onto the bed, then sails his*

*beret toward the clothes-rack in the corner. It falls on the
floor. He sits down on one of the cretonne-covered chairs,
and pulls his boots off. He leaves them standing, dripping,
in the middle of the floor and goes over to the bed. He
picks up his coat from the bed and throws it onto a chair.
It sprawls there. Then he lies down on the bed, pulls the
pillows out from under the cover to make a pile under
his head, and turns on the reading light. He reaches down,
opens the double door of the night table, by the bed, gets
out a bottle of whiskey, pours himself a drink into the
glass which had been placed neatly, top down, on top of
the water bottle, and splashes water into it. With the glass
in his left hand, he reaches over to the bookcase for a
book. He lies back a moment, still, then shrugs his shoulders and twists uncomfortably. Finally, he brings a pistol
out from underneath his belt band and lays it on the bed-
cover beside him. He draws his knees up, takes his first sip
of the drink, and commences to read]*

DOROTHY. [*From the next room*] Philip, Philip darling!
PHILIP. Yes.
DOROTHY. Come in here, please.
PHILIP. No, dear.
DOROTHY. I want to show you something.
PHILIP. [*Reading*] Bring it in here.
DOROTHY. All right, darling.

[*She takes a last look at the cape in the mirror. She is very
beautiful in it, and there is nothing wrong with the neck.
She comes in the door wearing the cape very proudly, and
turns with it, wearing it very gracefully and elegantly as
a model would*]

PHILIP. Where did you get that?
DOROTHY. I bought it, darling.
PHILIP. What with?
DOROTHY. Pesetas.
PHILIP. [*Coldly*] Very pretty.
DOROTHY. Don't you like it?
PHILIP. [*Still staring at the cape*] Very pretty.

DOROTHY. What's the matter, Philip?

PHILIP. Nothing.

DOROTHY. Don't you want me to have *anything* nice-looking?

PHILIP. That's absolutely your affair.

DOROTHY. But, *darling*. It's so cheap. The foxes only cost twelve hundred pesetas apiece.

PHILIP. That's one hundred and twenty days' pay for a man in the brigades. Let's see. That's four months. I don't believe I know any one who's been out four months without being hit—or killed.

DOROTHY. But, Philip, it doesn't have anything to do with the brigades. I bought pesetas at fifty to the dollar in Paris.

PHILIP. [*Coldly*] Really?

DOROTHY. Yes, darling. And why shouldn't I buy foxes if I want to? Some one has to buy them. They're there to be sold, and they come to less than twenty-two dollars a skin.

PHILIP. Marvellous, isn't it? How many foxes are there?

DOROTHY. About twelve. Oh, Philip, don't be cross.

PHILIP. You're doing quite well out of the war, aren't you? How did you smuggle your pesetas in?

DOROTHY. In a tin of Mum.

PHILIP. Mum, oh, yes, Mum. Mum's the word. And did the Mum take all the odor off them?

DOROTHY. Philip, you're acting *frightfully* moral!

PHILIP. I suppose I am frightfully moral, economically. I don't think even Mum, or what's the other lovely thing ladies use, Amolin is it?, would take the taint off those Black Bourse pesetas.

DOROTHY. If you're going to be unpleasant about it, I'll leave you.

PHILIP. Good!

[DOROTHY *starts out of the room, but turns at the door pleadingly*]

DOROTHY. But don't be unpleasant about it. Just be reasonable, and be pleased that I have such a lovely cape. Do you know what I was doing when you came in? I was thinking what we could do at just this time of day in Paris.

PHILIP. Paris?

DOROTHY. It will just be getting dark, and I meet you at the Ritz bar, and I'm wearing this cape. I'm sitting there waiting for you. You come in wearing a double-breasted guardsman's over-coat, very close fitting, a bowler hat, and you're carrying a stick.

PHILIP. You've been reading that American magazine, *Esquire*. You're not supposed to read what it says, you know. You're only supposed to look at the pictures.

DOROTHY. You order a whiskey with Perrier, and I have a champagne cocktail.

PHILIP. I don't like it.

DOROTHY. What?

PHILIP. The story. If you have to have day dreams, just keep me out of them, will you?

DOROTHY. It's just *playing*, darling.

PHILIP. Well, I don't play any more.

DOROTHY. But you did, darling. And we had lovely fun playing.

PHILIP. Just count me out now.

DOROTHY. But aren't we friends?

PHILIP. Oh, yes, you make all sorts of friends in a war.

DOROTHY. Darling, *please* stop it! Aren't we lovers?

PHILIP. Oh, that? Oh, certainly. Of course. Why not?

DOROTHY. But aren't we going to go and live together and have a lovely time and be happy? The way you say always in the night?

PHILIP. No. Not in a hundred thousand bloody years. Never believe what I say in the night. I lie like hell at night.

DOROTHY. But *why* can't we do what you say we'll do at night?

PHILIP. Because I'm in something where you don't go on and live together and have a lovely time and be happy.

DOROTHY. But why not?

PHILIP. Because, principally, I've discovered you're too busy. And secondly, it doesn't seem very important compared to any number of other things.

DOROTHY. But you're *never* busy!

PHILIP. [*He feels himself talking too much, but goes on*] No. But after this is over I'll get a course of discipline to rid me of any anarchistic habits I may have acquired. I'll probably be sent back to working with pioneers or something like that.

DOROTHY. I don't understand.

PHILIP. And because you don't understand, and you never could

understand, is the reason we're not going to go on and live together and have a lovely time and etcetera.

DOROTHY. Oh, it's worse than Skull and Bones.

PHILIP. What in God's name is Skull and Bones?

DOROTHY. It's a secret society a man belonged to one time that
I had just enough sense not to marry. It's very superior and
awfully good and worthy, and they take you in and tell you all
about it, just before the wedding, and when they told me about
it, I called the wedding off.

PHILIP. That's an excellent precedent.

DOROTHY. But can't we just go on now, as long as we have each
other, I mean if we aren't going to always keep on, and be nice
and enjoy what we have and not be bitter?

PHILIP. If you like.

DOROTHY. I'd like.

[*She has come over from the door and is standing by the
bed while they have been talking.* PHILIP *looks up at her,
then stands up, takes her in his arms and lifts her against
him onto the bed, silver foxes and all*]

PHILIP. They feel very fine and soft.

DOROTHY. They don't smell badly, do they?

PHILIP. [*His face over her shoulder in the foxes*] No, they don't
smell badly. And you feel lovely in them. And I love you, I don't
give a damn. I do. And it's only half-past five in the afternoon.

DOROTHY. And while we have it we can have it, can't we?

PHILIP. [*Shamelessly*] They feel really marvellously. I'm glad
you bought them.

[*He holds her very close*]

DOROTHY. We can have it now just this little while that we
have?

PHILIP. Yes. We'll have it.

[*There is a knock on the door and the handle turns to
admit* MAX. PHILIP *gets off the bed.* DOROTHY *remains
seated on it*]

MAX. I disturb? Yes?

PHILIP. No. Not at all. Max, this is an American comrade. Comrade Bridges. Comrade Max.

MAX. Salud, Comrade.

[*He goes over to the bed where* DOROTHY *is still seated and puts out his hand.* DOROTHY *shakes it and looks away*]

MAX. You are busy? Yes?

PHILIP. No. Not at all. Will you have a drink, Max?

MAX. No. Thank you.

PHILIP. ¿Hay novedades?

MAX. Algunas.

PHILIP. You won't have a drink?

MAX. No. Thank you very much.

DOROTHY. I'll go. Don't let me bother you.

PHILIP. There's no need to go.

DOROTHY. You'll come by later, perhaps.

PHILIP. Quite.

[*As she goes out* MAX *says with great politeness*]

MAX. Salud, Camarada.

DOROTHY. Salud.

[*She shuts the door between the two rooms before she goes out the regular door*]

MAX. [*When they are alone*] She is a Comrade?

PHILIP. No.

MAX. You introduced her as so.

PHILIP. Just a manner of speech. You call every one comrade in Madrid. All supposed to be working for the same cause.

MAX. It is not such a good manner of speech.

PHILIP. No. I suppose not. I seem to remember saying something like that myself once.

MAX. This girl, how do you call her? Britches?

PHILIP. Bridges.

MAX. She is something serious to you?

PHILIP. Serious?

MAX. Yes. You know what I mean.

PHILIP. I wouldn't say so. You could call her comic, rather. In some ways.

MAX. You spend much time with her?

PHILIP. A certain amount.

MAX. Whose time?

PHILIP. My time.

MAX. Never the Party's time?

PHILIP. My time is the Party's time.

MAX. That is what I mean. I am glad you understand so easily.

PHILIP. Oh, I understand very easily.

MAX. Do not be angry about something that is not you nor me.

PHILIP. I'm not angry. But I'm not supposed to be a damn monk.

MAX. Philip, Comrade. You have never been much like a damned monk.

PHILIP. No?

MAX. Nor does anybody expect you to be—ever.

PHILIP. No.

MAX. It is only a question of what interferes with your work. This girl—where does she come from? What is her background?

PHILIP. Ask her.

MAX. I suppose I will have to, then.

PHILIP. Haven't I done my work properly? Has any one complained?

MAX. Not until now.

PHILIP. And who complains now?

MAX. I complain now.

PHILIP. Yes?

MAX. Yes. I should have met you at Chicote's. If you were not there you should have left word for me. I go to Chicote's on time. You are not there. There is no word. I come here and find you with 'ner ganzen menagerie of silver foxes in your arms.

PHILIP. And you never want any of that?

MAX. Oh, yes. I want it all the time.

PHILIP. And what do *you* do?

MAX. Sometimes when I have time and I am not too tired, I find some one that will give me a little something while she looks the other way.

PHILIP. And you want it all the time?

MAX. I like very much. I am not a saint.

PHILIP. There *are* saints.

MAX. Yes. And others that are not. Only I am always very busy. Now we will talk of something else. Tonight we go again.

PHILIP. Good.

MAX. You want to go?

PHILIP. Look, I agree with you on the girl if you like; but don't be insulting to me. Don't get superior about work.

MAX. This girl is all right?

PHILIP. Oh, quite! She may be bad for me and I may waste time as you say and all that, but she's absolutely straight.

MAX. You are sure? You must remember I have never seen so many foxes.

PHILIP. She's a damned fool and all that, but she's as straight as I am!

MAX. And you are still straight?

PHILIP. I hope so. Does it show when you're not?

MAX. Oh, yes.

PHILIP. How do I look then?

[*He stands and looks at himself contemptuously in the glass.* MAX *looks at him and smiles very slowly. He nods his head*]

MAX. You look pretty straight to me.

PHILIP. You want to go in and question her about her background and all that?

MAX. No.

PHILIP. She has the same background all American girls have that come to Europe with a certain amount of money. They're all the same. Camps, college, money in family, now more or less than it was, usually less now, men, affairs, abortions, ambitions, and finally marry and settle down or don't marry and settle down. They open shops, or work in shops, some write, others play instruments, some go on the stage, some into films. They have something called the Junior League I believe that the virgins work at. All for the public good. This one writes. Quite well too, when she's not too lazy. Ask her about it all if you like. It's very dull though, I tell you.

MAX. I am not interested.

PHILIP. I thought you were.

MAX. No. I think it over and I leave it all to you.

PHILIP. All what to me?

MAX. All about this girl. To deal with as you should.

PHILIP. I wouldn't have too much confidence in me.

MAX. I have confidence in you.

PHILIP. [*Bitterly*] I wouldn't have too much. Sometimes I'm damned tired of it. Of the whole damned business. So I hate it.

MAX. Of course.

PHILIP. Yes. And now you'll talk me out of it. I murdered that bloody young Wilkinson the other day. Just through carelessness. Don't tell me I didn't.

MAX. Now you talk nonsense. But you were not as careful as you should have been.

PHILIP. It was my fault he was killed. I left him in there in the room in my chair with the door open. That wasn't where I was going to use him.

MAX. You did not leave him there on purpose. You must not think about it now that it is over.

PHILIP. No—just a deathtrap set from carelessness.

MAX. He would probably have been killed later anyway.

PHILIP. Oh, yes. Of course. That makes it marvellous, doesn't it? That's perfectly splendid. I suppose I didn't know that, either.

MAX. I have seen you in such a mood before. I know you will be all right again.

PHILIP. Yes. But you know how I'll be when I'm all right? I'll have a dozen drinks in me and I'll be with some tart. Very jolly I'll be. That's your idea of all right with me.

MAX. No.

PHILIP. I'm fed up with it. You know where I'd like to be? At some place like Saint Tropez on the Riviera, waking up in the morning with no bloody war, and a café crème with proper milk in it . . . and *brioches* with fresh strawberry jam, and *œufs au jambon* all on one tray.

MAX. And the girl?

PHILIP. Yes, and the girl, too. You're damned right, the girl. Silver foxes and all.

MAX. I told you she was bad for you.

PHILIP. Or good for me. I've been doing this so long I'm bloody well fed up with it. With all of it.

MAX. You do it so *every one* will have a good breakfast like that. You do it so *no one* will ever be hungry. You do it so men will not have to fear ill health or old age; so they can live and work in dignity and not as slaves.

PHILIP. Yes. Sure. I know.

MAX. You know why you do it. And if you have a little *défaillance* I understand.

PHILIP. This one was a pretty big *défaillance*, and I've had it a long time. Ever since I saw the girl. You don't know what they do to you.

[*There is the incoming scream of a shell and the sound of its burst in the street. You hear a child scream; first high, then in short, sharp, thin cries. You hear people running in the street. Another shell comes in.* PHILIP *has opened the windows wide. After the burst you hear the sound of people running again*]

MAX. You do it to stop *that* forever.

PHILIP. The swine! They timed it for the minute the cinemas are out.

[*Another shell comes in and bursts, and you hear a dog go yelping down the street*]

MAX. You hear? You do it for all men. You do it for the children. And sometimes you do it even for dogs. Go in and see the girl a while now. She needs you now.

PHILIP. No. Let her take it by herself. She's got her silver foxes. The hell with it all.

MAX. No. Go in now. She needs you now.

[*Another shell comes in with a long swishing rush, and bursts outside in the street. There is no running and no noise after this one*]

MAX. I lie down now for a while here. Go in to her now.

PHILIP. All right. Sure. Anything you say. I do whatever you say.

[*He starts for the door and opens it as there is another inrushing, down-dropping, whishing sound and another burst; beyond the hotel this time*]

MAX. It is just a little bombardment. The big one is for tonight.

[PHILIP *opens the door of the other room. Through the door you hear* PHILIP *speak, in a flat voice*]

PHILIP. Hello, Bridges. How are you?

CURTAIN

ACT THREE · SCENE TWO

Interior of an artillery observation post in a shelled house on the top of the Extremadura road.

It is located in the tower of what has been a very pretentious house and access to it is by a ladder which replaces the circular iron stairway which has been smashed and hangs, broken and twisted. You see the ladder against the tower and at its top, the back of the observation post which faces toward Madrid. It is night and the sacks which plug its windows have been removed and looking out through them you see nothing but darkness because the lights of Madrid have been extinguished. There are large-scale military maps on the walls with the positions marked with colored tacks and tapes, and on a plain table there is a field telephone. There is an extra large size, single, German model, long tube telemeter opposite the narrow opening in the wall to the right of the table and a chair beside it. There is an ordinary-sized double tube telemeter at the other opening with a chair at its base. There is another plain table with a telephone on the right of the room. At the foot of the ladder is a SENTRY *with fixed bayonet, and at the top of the ladder in the room, where there is just enough height for him to stand straight with his rifle and bayonet, there is another* SENTRY. *As the curtain rises, you see the scene as described with the* TWO SENTRIES *at their posts. Two* SIGNALLERS *are bending over the larger table. After the curtain is up, you see the lights of a motor which shine brightly on the ladder at the base of the tower. They come closer and closer and almost blind the* SENTRY.

SENTRY. Cut those lights!

[*The lights shine on, illuminating the* SENTRY *with a blinding light*]

SENTRY. [*Presenting his rifle, pulling back the bolt, and shoving it forward with a click*] Cut those lights!

[*He says it very slowly, clearly and dangerously, and it is obvious that he will fire. The lights go off and* THREE MEN, *two of them in officer's uniform, one large and stout, the other rather thin and elegantly dressed, with riding boots which shine in the flashlight the stout man carries, and a* CIVILIAN, *cross the stage from the left where they have left the motor car off stage; and approach the ladder*]

SENTRY. [*Giving the first half of the password*] The Victory——
THIN OFFICER. [*Snappily and disdainfully*] To those who deserve it.
SENTRY. Pass.
THIN OFFICER. [*To* CIVILIAN] Just climb up here.
CIVILIAN. I've been here before.

[*The three of them climb the ladder. At the top of the ladder the* SENTRY, *seeing the insignia on the cap of the large, stout officer, presents arms. The* SIGNALLERS *remain seated at their telephones. The large officer goes over to the table followed by the* CIVILIAN *and the shiny-booted officer who is obviously his* AIDE]

LARGE OFFICER. What's the matter with these signallers?
AIDE. [*To* SIGNALLERS] Come along! Stand to attention there! What's the matter with you?

[SIGNALLERS *stand to attention rather wearily*]

At ease!

[*The* SIGNALLERS *sit down. The* LARGE OFFICER *is studying the map. The* CIVILIAN *looks out of the telemeter and sees nothing in the darkness*]

CIVILIAN. The bombardment's for midnight?

AIDE. What time is the shoot for, Sir?

[*Speaking to the* LARGE OFFICER]

LARGE OFFICER. [*Speaking with a German accent*] You talk too much!

AIDE. I'm sorry, sir. Would you care to have a look at these?

[*He hands him a sheaf of typed orders clipped together.* LARGE OFFICER *takes them and glances at them. Hands them back*]

LARGE OFFICER. [*In heavy voice*] I am familiar with them. I wrote them.

AIDE. Quite, sir. I thought perhaps you wished to verify them.

LARGE OFFICER. I heff verified them!

[*One of the phones rings.* SIGNALLER *at table takes it and listens*]

SIGNALLER. Yes. No. Yes. All right.

[*He nods to the* LARGE OFFICER]

For you, sir.

[LARGE OFFICER *takes the phone*]

LARGE OFFICER. Hello. Yes. That is right. Are you a fool? No? As ordered. By salvos means by salvos.

[*He hangs up the receiver and looks at his watch*]
[*To* AIDE]

What time have you?

AIDE. Twelve minus one, sir.

LARGE OFFICER. I deal with fools here. You cannot say that you command where there is no discipline. Signallers who sit at table when a General comes in. Artillery brigadiers who ask for explanations of orders. What time did you say it was?

AIDE. [*Looking at his watch*] Twelve minus thirty seconds, sir.

SIGNALLER. The brigade called six times, sir!

LARGE OFFICER. [*Lighting a cigar*] What time?

AIDE. Minus fifteen, sir.

LARGE OFFICER. What minus fifteen what?
AIDE. Twelve minus fifteen seconds, sir.

[*Just then you hear the guns. They are a very different sound from the incoming shells. There is a sharp, cracking boom, boom, boom, boom, as a kettle drum would make struck sharply before a microphone and then whish, whish, whish, whish, chu, chu, chu, chu, chu—chu—as the shells go away followed by a distant burst. Another battery closer and louder commences firing and then they are firing all along the line in quick, pounding thuds and the air is full of the noise the departing projectiles make. Through the open window you see the skyline of Madrid lit now by the flashes. The LARGE OFFICER is standing at the big telemeter. The CIVILIAN at the two-branched one. The AIDE is looking over the CIVILIAN's shoulder*]

CIVILIAN. God, what a beautiful sight!
AIDE. We'll kill plenty of them tonight. The Marxist bastards. This catches them in their holes.
CIVILIAN. It's wonderful to see it.
GENERAL. Is it satisfactory?

[*He does not remove his eyes from the telemeter*]

CIVILIAN. It's beautiful! How long will it go on?
GENERAL. We're giving them an hour. Then ten minutes without. Then fifteen minutes more.
CIVILIAN. No shells will light in the Salamanca quarter, will they? That's where nearly all our people are.
GENERAL. A few will land there.
CIVILIAN. But why?
GENERAL. Errors by Spanish batteries.
CIVILIAN. Why by Spanish batteries?
GENERAL. Spanish batteries are not so good as ours.

[*The CIVILIAN does not answer and the firing keeps up although the batteries are not firing with the speed with which they commenced. There is an incoming whistling rush, then a roar, and a shell has landed just short of the observation post*]

GENERAL. They answer now a little.

[*There are no lights in the observation post now except that of the gun flashes and the light of the cigarette the* SENTRY *at the foot of the ladder is smoking. As you watch you see the glow of this cigarette describe half an arc in the dark, and there is a thud clearly heard by the audience as the* SENTRY *falls. You hear the sound of two blows. Another shell comes in with the same sort of screaming rush, and at its burst you see in the flash two men climbing the ladder*]

GENERAL. [*Speaking from the telemeter*] Ring me Garabitas.

[SIGNALLER *rings. Then rings again*]

SIGNALLER. Sorry, sir. The wire's gone.
GENERAL. [*To the other* SIGNALLER] Get me through to the Division.
SIGNALLER. I have no wire, sir.
GENERAL. Put some one to trace your wire!
SIGNALLER. Yes, sir.

[*He rises in the dark*]

GENERAL. What's that man smoking for? What sort of an army out of the chorus of *Carmen* is this?

[*You see the cigarette in the mouth of the* SENTRY *at the top of the ladder describe a long parabola toward the ground as though he had tossed it away, and there is the solid noise of a body falling. A flashlight illuminates the three men by the telemeters and the two* SIGNALLERS]

PHILIP. [*From inside the open door at the top of the ladder. In a low, very quiet voice*] Put your hands up and don't try anything heroic, or I'll blow your heads off!

[*He is holding a short automatic rifle which was slung over his back as he climbed up the ladder*]

I mean all five of you! *KEEP* them up there, you fat bastard!

[MAX *has a hand grenade in his right hand, the flashlight in his left*]

MAX. You make a noise, you move, and everybody is dead. You hear?

PHILIP. Who do you want?

MAX. Only the fat one and the townsman. Tie me up the rest. You have also good adhesive tape?

PHILIP. *Da.*

MAX. You see. We are all Russians. Everybody is Russians in Madrid! Hurry up, Tovarich, and tape good the mouths, because I have to throw this thing before we go. You see the pin is pulled already!

[*Just before the curtain goes down, as* PHILIP *is advancing toward them with the short automatic rifle, you see the men's white faces in the flashlight. The batteries are still firing. From below and beyond the house comes a voice—* "Cut out that light!"]

MAX. O.K. soldier, in just a minute!

CURTAIN

ACT THREE · SCENE THREE

As the curtain rises you see the same room in Seguridad headquarters that was shown in Act II, Scene I. ANTONIO, *of the Comisariato de Vigilancia, is sitting behind the table.* PHILIP *and* MAX, *muddy and much the worse for wear, are seated in the two chairs.* PHILIP *still has the automatic rifle slung over his back. The* CIVILIAN *from the observation post, his beret gone, his trench coat ripped clean up the back, one sleeve hanging loose, is standing before the table with an* ASSAULT GUARD *on either side of him.*

ANTONIO. [*To the two* ASSAULT GUARDS] You can go!

[*They salute. and go out to the right, carrying their rifles at trail*]
[*To* PHILIP]

What became of the other?

PHILIP. We lost him coming in.

MAX. He was too heavy and he would not walk.

ANTONIO. It would have been a wonderful capture.

PHILIP. You can't do these things as they do them in the cinema.

ANTONIO. Still, if we could have had him!

PHILIP. I'll draw you a little map and you can send out there and find him.

ANTONIO. Yes?

MAX. He was a soldier and he would never have talked. I would have liked the questioning of him, but such a business is useless.

PHILIP. When we're through here I'll draw you a little map and you can send out for him. No one will have moved him. We left him in a likely spot.

CIVILIAN. [*In an hysterical voice*] You *murdered* him.

PHILIP. [*Contemptuously*] Shut up, will you?

MAX. I promise you, he would not have ever talked. I know such men.

PHILIP. You see, we didn't expect to find two of these sportsmen at the same time. And this other specimen was oversized and he wouldn't walk finally. He made a sort of sit-down strike. And I don't know whether you've ever tried coming in at night from up there. There are a couple of very odd spots. So you see we didn't really have any bloody choice in the matter.

CIVILIAN. [*Hysterically*] So you murdered him! I saw you do it.

PHILIP. Just quiet down, will you? No one asked you for your opinion.

MAX. You want us now?

ANTONIO. No.

MAX. I think I like to go. This isn't what I like very much. It makes too much remember.

PHILIP. You need me?

ANTONIO. No.

PHILIP. You don't need to worry. You'll get everything—the lists, the locations, everything. This thing has been running it.

ANTONIO. Yes.

PHILIP. You don't need to worry about his talking. He's the talkative type.

ANTONIO. He is a politician. Yes. I have talked to many politicians.

CIVILIAN. [*Hysterically*] You'll never make me talk! Never! Never! Never!

[MAX *and* PHILIP *look at each other*—PHILIP *grins*]

PHILIP. [*Very quietly*] You're talking now. Haven't you noticed it?

CIVILIAN. No! No!

MAX. If it is all right I will go.

[*He stands up*]

PHILIP. I'll run along too, I think.

ANTONIO. You do not want to stay to hear it?

MAX. Please, no.

ANTONIO. It will be very interesting.

PHILIP. It's that we are tired.

ANTONIO. It will be very interesting.

PHILIP. I'll be by tomorrow.

ANTONIO. I would like you very much to stay.

MAX. Please. If you do not mind. As a favor.

CIVILIAN. What are you going to do to me?

ANTONIO. Nothing. Only that you should answer some questions.

CIVILIAN. I'll never talk.

ANTONIO. Oh, yes, you will!

MAX. Please. Please. I go now!

CURTAIN

ACT THREE · SCENE FOUR

Same as Act I, Scene III, but it is late afternoon. As the curtain rises, you see the two rooms. DOROTHY BRIDGES' *room is dark.* PHILIP'S *is lighted, with the curtains drawn.* PHILIP *is lying face down on the bed.* ANITA *is sitting on a chair by the bed.*

ANITA. Philip!

PHILIP. [*Not turning or looking toward her*] What's the matter?

ANITA. Please, Philip.

PHILIP. Please bloody what?

ANITA. Where is whiskey?

PHILIP. Under the bed.

ANITA. Thank you.

[*She looks under the bed. Then crawls part way under*]

No find.

PHILIP. Try the closet then. Somebody's been in here cleaning up again.

ANITA. [*Goes to the closet and opens it. She looks carefully inside*] Is all empty bottles.

PHILIP. You're just a little discoverer. Come here.

ANITA. I want find a whiskey.

PHILIP. Look in the night table.

[ANITA *goes over to the night table by the bed and opens the door—she brings out a bottle of whiskey. Goes for a glass into the bathroom, and pours a whiskey into it and adds water from the carafe by the bed*]

ANITA. Philip. Drink this feel better.

[PHILIP *sits up and looks at her*]

PHILIP. Hello, Black Beauty. How did you get in here?

ANITA. From the pass key.

PHILIP. Well.

ANITA. I no see you. I plenty worried. I come here they say you inside. I knock door no answer. I knock more. No answer. I say open me up with the pass key.

PHILIP. And they did?

ANITA. I said you sent for me.

PHILIP. Did I?

ANITA. No.

PHILIP. Thoughtful of you to come though.

ANITA. Philip you still that big blonde?

PHILIP. I don't know. I'm sort of mixed up about that. Things are getting sort of complicated. Every night I ask her to marry me, and every morning I tell her I don't mean it. I think, probably, things can't go on like that. No. They can't go on like that.

[ANITA *sits down by him and pats his head and smooths his hair back*]

ANITA. You feel plenty bad. I know.

PHILIP. Want me to tell you a secret?

ANITA. Yes.

PHILIP. I never felt worse.

ANITA. Is a disappoint. Was think you tell how you catch all the people of the Fifth Column.

PHILIP. I didn't catch them. Only caught one man. Disgusting specimen he was, too.

[*There is a knock on the door. It is the* MANAGER]

MANAGER. Excuse profoundly if disturbation——

PHILIP. Keep it clean you know. There's ladies present.

MANAGER. I mean only to enter and see if every *thing* in order. Control possible actions of young lady in case your absence or incapacity. Also desire offer sincerest warmest greetings congratulations admirable performance feat of counterespionage resulting announcement evening papers arrest three hundred members Fifth Column.

PHILIP. That's in the paper?

MANAGER. With details of arrestations of every type of reprehensible engaged in shooting, plotting assassinations—sabotaging, communicating with enemy, every form of delights.

PHILIP. Of delights?

MANAGER. Is a French word, spells out D-E-L-I-T-S, meaning offenses.

PHILIP. And that's all in the paper?

MANAGER. Absolutely, Mr. Philip.

PHILIP. And where do I come in?

MANAGER. Oh, everybody knows you were engaged in prosecution of such investigations.

PHILIP. Just how do they know?

MANAGER. [*Reproachfully*] Mr. Philip. Is Madrid. In Madrid everybody knows everything often before occurrence of same. After occurrence sometimes is discussions as to who actually did. But before occurrence all the world knows clearly who must do. I offer congratulations now in order to precede reproaches of unsatisfiables who ask, "Ah ha! Only 300? Where are the others?"

PHILIP. Don't be so gloomy. I suppose I'll have to be leaving now though.

MANAGER. Mr. Philip, I have thought of that and I come here, make what hope will result as excellent proposition. If you leave is useless to carry tinned goods as baggage.

[*There is a knock on the door. It is* MAX]

MAX. Salud camaradas.
EVERY ONE. Salud.
PHILIP. [*To* MANAGER] Run along now, Comrade Stamp Collector. We can talk about that later.
MAX. [*To* PHILIP] *Wie gehts?*
PHILIP. *Gut.* Not too *gut.*
ANITA. O.K. I take bath?
PHILIP. More than O.K., darling. But keep the door shut, will you?
ANITA. [*From bathroom*] Is warm water.
PHILIP. That's a good sign. Shut the door, please.

[ANITA *shuts the door.* MAX *comes over by the bed and sits down on a chair.* PHILIP *is sitting on the bed with his legs hanging over*]

PHILIP. Want anything?
MAX. No, Comrade. You were there?
PHILIP. Oh, yes. I stayed all through it. Every bit of it. All of it. They needed to know something and they called me back.
MAX. How was he?
PHILIP. Cowardly. But it only came out a little at a time for a while.
MAX. And then?
PHILIP. Oh, and then finally he was spilling it out faster than a stenographer could take it. I have a strong stomach, you know.
MAX [*Ignoring this*] I see in the paper about the arrests. Why do they publish such things?
PHILIP. I don't know, my boy. Why do they? I'll bite.
MAX. It is good for morale. But it is also very good to get every one. Did they bring in—the—ah——
PHILIP. Oh, yes. The corpse you mean? They fetched him in from where we left him, and Antonio had him placed in a chair in the corner and I put a cigarette in his mouth and lit it and it

was all very jolly. Only the cigarette wouldn't stay lighted, of course.

MAX. I am very happy I did not have to stay.

PHILIP. I stayed. And then I left. And then I came back. Then I left and they called me back again. I've been there until an hour ago and now I'm through. For today, that is. Finished my work for the day. Something else to do tomorrow.

MAX. We did very good job.

PHILIP. As good as we could. It was very brilliant and very flashy, and there were probably many holes in the net and a big part of the haul got away. But they can haul again. You have to send me some place else though. I'm no good here any more. Too many people know what I'm doing. *Not* because I talk, either. It just gets that way.

MAX. There are many places to send. But you still have some work to do here.

PHILIP. I know. But ship me out as quickly as you can, will you? I'm getting on the jumpy side.

MAX. What about the girl in the other room?

PHILIP. Oh, I'm going to break it off with her.

MAX. I do not ask that.

PHILIP. No. But you would sooner or later. There's no sense babying me along. We're in for fifty years of undeclared wars and I've signed up for the duration. I don't exactly remember when it was, but I signed up all right.

MAX. So have we all. There is no question of signing. There is no need to talk with bitterness.

PHILIP. I'm not bitter. I just don't want to fool myself. Nor let things get a hold in part of me where no things should get hold. This thing was getting pretty well in. Well, I know how to cure it.

MAX. How?

PHILIP. I'll show you how.

MAX. Remember, Philip, I am a kind man.

PHILIP. Oh, quite. So am I. You ought to watch me work sometime.

[*While they have been talking you see the door of 109 open and* DOROTHY BRIDGES *comes in. She turns up the*

*lights, takes off her street coat and puts on the silver fox
cape. Standing, she turns in it before the mirror. She looks
very beautiful this evening. She goes to the phonograph
and puts on the Chopin Mazurka and sits in a chair by the
reading light with a book]*

PHILIP. There she is. She's come, what do you call the place,
home—now.

MAX. Philip, Comrade, you do not have to. I tell you truly I see
no signs that she interferes with your work in any way.

PHILIP. No, but I do. And you would damned soon.

MAX. I leave it to you as before. But remember to be kind. To
us to whom dreadful things have been done, kindness in all
possible things is of great importance.

PHILIP. I'm very kind, too, you know. Oh, am I kind! I'm
terrific!

MAX. No, I do not know that you are kind. I would like you
to be.

PHILIP. Just wait in here, will you?

[PHILIP *goes out of the door and knocks on the door of
109. He pushes it open after knocking and goes in]*

DOROTHY. Hello, beloved.

PHILIP. Hello. How have you been?

DOROTHY. I'm very well and very happy now you're here.
Where have you been? You never came in last night. Oh, I'm so
glad you're here.

PHILIP. Have you a drink?

DOROTHY. Yes, darling.

[*She makes him a whiskey and water. In the other room*
MAX *is sitting in a chair staring at the electric stove]*

DOROTHY. Where were you, Philip?

PHILIP. Just around. Checking up on things.

DOROTHY. And how were things?

PHILIP. Some were good, you know. And some were not so
good. I suppose they evened up.

DOROTHY. And you don't have to go out tonight?

PHILIP. I don't know.

DOROTHY. Philip, beloved, what's the matter?

PHILIP. Nothing's the matter.

DOROTHY. Philip, let's go away from here. I don't have to stay here. I've sent away three articles. We could go to that place near Saint Tropez and the rains haven't started yet and it would be lovely there now with no people. Then afterwards we could go to ski.

PHILIP. [*Very bitterly*] Yes, and afterwards to Egypt and make love happily in all the hotels, and a thousand breakfasts come up on trays in the thousand fine mornings of the next three years; or the ninety of the next three months; or however long it took you to be tired of me, or me of you. And all we'd do would be amuse ourselves. We'd stay at the Crillon, or the Ritz, and in the fall when the leaves were off the trees in the Bois and it was sharp and cold, we'd drive out to Auteuil steeplechasing, and keep warm by those big coal braziers in the paddock, and watch them take the water jump and see them coming over the bullfinch and the old stone wall. That's it. And nip into the bar for a champagne cocktail and afterwards ride back in to dinner at La Rue's and weekends go to shoot pheasants in the Sologne. Yes, yes, that's it. And fly out to Nairobi and the old Mathaiga Club, and in the spring a little spot of salmon fishing. Yes, yes, that's it. And every night in bed together. Is that it?

DOROTHY. Oh, darling, think how it would be! Have you *that* much money?

PHILIP. I did have. Till I got into this business.

DOROTHY. And we'll do all that and Saint Moritz, too?

PHILIP. Saint Moritz? Don't be vulgar. Kitzbühel you mean. You meet people like Michael Arlen at Saint Moritz.

DOROTHY. But you wouldn't have to meet him, darling. You could cut him. And will we really do all that?

PHILIP. Do you want to?

DOROTHY. Oh, darling!

PHILIP. Would you like to go to Hungary, too, some fall? You can take an estate there very cheaply and only pay for what you shoot. And on the Danube flats you have great flights of geese. And have you ever been to Lamu where the long white beach is, with the dhows beached on their sides, and the wind in the palms at night? Or what about Malindi where you can surfboard on the beach and the northeast monsoon cool and fresh, and no pajamas, and no sheets at night. You'd like Malindi.

DOROTHY. I know I would, Philip.

PHILIP. And have you ever been out to the Sans Souci in Havana on a Saturday night to dance in the Patio under the royal palms? They're gray and they rise like columns and you stay up all night there and play dice, or the wheel, and drive in to Jaimanitas for breakfast in the daylight. And everybody knows every one else and it's very pleasant and gay.

DOROTHY. Can we go there?

PHILIP. No.

DOROTHY. Why not, Philip?

PHILIP. We won't go anywhere.

DOROTHY. Why not, darling?

PHILIP. You can go if you like. I'll draw you up an itinerary.

DOROTHY. But why can't we go together?

PHILIP. You can go. But I've been to all those places and I've left them all behind. And where I go now I go alone, or with others who go there for the same reason I go.

DOROTHY. And I can't go there?

PHILIP. No.

DOROTHY. And why can't I go wherever it is? I could learn and I'm *not* afraid.

PHILIP. One reason is I don't know where it is. And another is I wouldn't take you.

DOROTHY. Why not?

PHILIP. Because you're useless, really. You're uneducated, you're useless, you're a fool and you're lazy.

DOROTHY. Maybe the others. But I'm not useless.

PHILIP. Why aren't you useless?

DOROTHY. You know—or you ought to know.

[*She is crying*]

PHILIP. Oh, yes. *That.*

DOROTHY. Is that all it means to you?

PHILIP. That's a commodity you shouldn't pay too high a price for.

DOROTHY. So I'm a commodity?

PHILIP. Yes, a very handsome commodity. The most beautiful I ever had.

DOROTHY. Good. I'm glad to hear you say it. And I'm glad it's daylight. Now get out of here. You conceited, *conceited* drunkard. You ridiculous, puffed-up, posing braggart. You commodity, you. Did it ever occur to you that you're a commodity, too? A commodity one shouldn't pay too high a price for?

PHILIP. [*Laughing*] No. But I see it the way you put it.

DOROTHY. Well, you are. You're a perfectly vicious commodity. Never home. Out all night. Dirty, muddy, disorderly. You're a *terrible* commodity. I just liked the package it was put up in. That was all. I'm glad you're going away.

PHILIP. Really?

DOROTHY. Yes, *really*. You and your commodity. But you didn't have to mention all those places if we weren't ever going to them.

PHILIP. I'm very sorry. That wasn't kind.

DOROTHY. Oh, don't be kind either. You're frightful when you're kind. Only kind people should try being kind. You're horrible when you're kind. And you didn't have to mention them in the daytime.

PHILIP. I'm sorry.

DOROTHY. Oh, don't be sorry. You're at your *worst* when you're sorry. I can't *stand* you sorry. Just get out.

PHILIP. Well, good-bye.

[*He puts his arms around her to kiss her*]

DOROTHY. Don't kiss me either. You'll kiss me and then you'll go right in to commodities. I know you.

[PHILIP *holds her tight and kisses her*]

Oh, Philip, Philip, Philip.

PHILIP. Good-bye.

DOROTHY. You—you—you don't want the commodity?

PHILIP. I can't afford it.

[DOROTHY *twists away from him*]

DOROTHY. Then, go then.

PHILIP. Good-bye.

DOROTHY. Oh, get out.

[PHILIP *goes out the door and into his room.* MAX *is still sitting in the chair. In the other room* DOROTHY *rings the bell for the maid*]

MAX. So?

[PHILIP *stands there looking into the electric stove.* MAX *looks into the stove too. In the other room* PETRA *has come to the door*]

PETRA. Yes, Señorita.

[DOROTHY *is sitting on the bed. Her head is up but there are tears running down her cheeks.* PETRA *goes over to her*]

What is it, Señorita?

DOROTHY. Oh, Petra, he's bad just as you said he was. He's bad, bad, bad. And like a damn fool I thought we were going to be happy. But he's bad.

PETRA. Yes, Señorita.

DOROTHY. But oh, Petra, the trouble is I *love* him.

[PETRA *stands there by the bed with* DOROTHY. *In Room 110* PHILIP *stands in front of the night table. He pours himself a whiskey and puts water in it*]

PHILIP. Anita.

ANITA. [*From inside the bathroom*] Yes, Philip.

PHILIP. Anita, come out whenever you've finished your bath.

MAX. I go.

PHILIP. No. Stay around.

MAX. No. No. No. Please, I go.

PHILIP. [*In a very dry flat voice*] Anita, was the water hot?

ANITA. [*From inside the bathroom*] Was lovely bath.

MAX. I go. Please, please, please, I go.

CURTAIN

The Denunciation

The Butterfly and the Tank

Night Before Battle

Under the Ridge

Story takes place the winter of 1937-38.
Story is narrated sometime after May 1938.
Composed May - Sept. 1938
Pub. Esquire, Nov. 1938

The Denunciation   *Chicote*

Narrator = Henry Emmunds   Story # 1

Chicote's in the old days in Madrid was a place sort of like The Stork, without the music and the debutantes, or the Waldorf's men's bar if they let girls in. You know, they came in, but it was a man's place and they didn't have any status. Pedro Chicote was the proprietor and he had one of those personalities that make a place. He was a great bartender and he was always pleasant, always cheerful, and he had a lot of zest. Now zest is a rare enough thing and few people have it for long. It should not be confused with showmanship either. Chicote had it and it was not faked or put on. He was also modest, simple and friendly. He really was as nice and pleasant and still as marvelously efficient as George, the chasseur at the Ritz bar in Paris, which is about the strongest comparison you can make to anyone who has been around, and he ran a fine bar.

In those days the snobs among the rich young men of Madrid hung out at something called the Nuevo Club and the good guys went to Chicote's. A lot of people went there that I did not like, the same as at The Stork, say, but I was never in Chicote's that it wasn't pleasant. One reason was that you did not talk politics *i.e., in* there. There were cafés where you went for politics and nothing *the old* else but you didn't talk politics at Chicote's. You talked plenty *days* of the other five subjects though and in the evening the best looking girls in the town showed up there and it was the place to start an evening from, all right, and we had all started some fine ones from there.

Then it was the place where you dropped in to find out who was in town, or where they had gone to if they were out of town. And if it was summer, and there was no one in town, you could always sit and enjoy a drink because the waiters were all pleasant.

It was like a club only you didn't have to pay any dues and you could pick a girl up there. It was the best bar in Spain, certainly, and I think one of the best bars in the world, and all of us that used to hang out there had a great affection for it.

Another thing was that the drinks were wonderful. If you ordered a Martini it was made with the best gin that money could buy, and Chicote had a barrel whiskey that came from Scotland that was so much better than the advertised brands that it was pitiful to compare it with ordinary Scotch. Well, when the revolt started, Chicote was up at San Sebastian running the summer place he had there. He is still running it and they say it is the best bar in Franco's Spain. The waiters took over the Madrid place and they are still running it, but the good liquor is all gone now.

Most of Chicote's old customers are on Franco's side; but some of them are on the Government side. Because it was a very cheerful place, and because really cheerful people are usually the bravest, and the bravest get killed quickest, a big part of Chicote's old customers are now dead. The barrel whiskey has all been gone for many months now and we finished the last of the yellow gin in May of 1938. There's not much there to go for now so I suppose Luis Delgado, if he had come to Madrid a little later, might have stayed away from there and not gotten into that trouble. But when he came to Madrid in the month of November of 1937 they still had the yellow gin and they still had Indian Quinine water. They do not seem worth risking your life for, so maybe he just wanted to have a drink in the old place. Knowing him, and knowing the place in the old days it would be perfectly understandable.

They had butchered a cow at the Embassy that day and the porter had called up at the Hotel Florida to tell us that they had saved us ten pounds of fresh meat. I walked over to get it through the early dusk of a Madrid winter. Two assault guards with rifles sat on chairs outside the Embassy gate and the meat was waiting at the porter's lodge.

The porter said it was a very good cut but that the cow was lean. I offered him some roasted sunflower seeds and some acorns from the pocket of my mackinaw jacket and we joked a little standing outside the lodge on the gravel of the Embassy drive-way.

I walked home across the town with the meat heavy under my arm. They were shelling up the Gran Via and I went into Chicote's to wait it out. It was noisy and crowded and I sat at a little table in one corner against the sandbagged window with the meat on the bench beside me and drank a gin and tonic water. It was that week that we discovered they still had tonic water. No one had ordered any since the war started and it was still the same price as before the revolt. The evening papers were not yet out so I bought three party tracts from an old woman. They were ten centavos apiece and I told her to keep the change from a peseta. She said God would bless me. I doubted this but read the three leaflets and drank the gin and tonic.

#1

A waiter I had known in the old days came over to the table and said something to me.

"No," I said. "I don't believe it."

"Yes," he insisted, slanting his tray and his head in the same direction. "Don't look now. There he is."

"It's not my business," I told him.

"Nor mine either."

He went away and I bought the evening papers which had just come in from another old woman and read them. There was no doubt about the man the waiter had pointed out. We both knew him very well. All I could think was; the fool. The utter bloody fool.

Just then a Greek comrade came over and sat down at the table. He was a company commander in the Fifteenth Brigade who had been buried by an airplane bomb which had killed four other men and he had been sent in to be under observation for a while and then sent to a rest home or something of the sort.

"How are you John?" I asked him. "Try one of these."

"What you call that drink, Mr. Emmunds?"

"Gin and tonic."

"What is that kind of tonic?"

"Quinine. Try one."

"Listen I don't drink very much but is a quinine very good for fever. I try little one."

"What did the doctor say about you John?"

"Is a no necessity see doctor. I am all right. Only I have like buzzing noises all the time in the head."

"You have to go to see him, John."

"I go all right. But he not understand. He says I have no papers to admit."

"I'll call up about it," I said. "I know the people there. Is the doctor a German?"

"That's right," said John. "Is a German. No talk English very good."

Just then the waiter came over. He was an old man with a bald head and very old-fashioned manners which the war had not changed. He was very worried.

"I have a son at the front," he said. "I have another son killed. Now about this."

"It is thy problem."

"And you? Already I have told you."

"I came in here to have a drink before eating."

"And I work here. But tell me."

"It is thy problem," I said. "I am not a politician."

"Do you understand Spanish, John?" I asked the Greek comrade.

"No, I understand few words but I speak Greek, English, Arabic. One time I speak good Arabic. Listen you know how I get buried?"

"No. I knew you were buried. That's all."

He had a dark good-looking face and very dark hands that he moved about when he talked. He came from one of the islands and he spoke with great intensity.

"Well, I tell you now. You see I have very much experience in war. Before I am Captain in Greek army too. I am good soldier. So when I see plane come over there when we are in trenches there at Fuentes del Ebro I look at him close. I look at plane come over, bank, turn like this (he turned and banked with his hands), look down on us and I say, 'Ah ha. Is for the General Staff. Is made the observation. Pretty soon come others.'

"So just like I say come others. So I am stand there and watch. I watch close. I look up and I point out to company what happens. Is come three and three. One first and two behind. Is pass one group of three and I say to company, 'See? Now is pass one formation.'

"Is pass the other three and I say to company, 'Now is hokay. Now is all right. Now is nothing more to worry.' That the last thing I remember for two weeks."

"When did it happen?"

"About one month ago. You see is my helmet forced down over my face when am buried by bomb so I have the air in that helmet to breathe until they dig me out but I know nothing about that. But in that air I breathe is the smoke from the explosion and that make me sick for long time. Now am I hokay, only with the ringing in the head. What you call this drink?"

"Gin and tonic. Schweppes Indian tonic water. This was a very fancy café before the war and this used to cost five pesetas when there were only seven pesetas to the dollar. We just found out they still have the tonic water and they're charging the same price for it. There's only a case left."

"Is a good drink all right. Tell me, how was this city before the war?"

"Fine. Like now only lots to eat."

The waiter came over and leaned toward the table.

"And if I don't?" he said. "It is my responsibility."

"If you wish to, go to the telephone and call this number. Write it down."

He wrote it down. "Ask for Pepé," I said.

"I have nothing against him," the waiter said. "But it is the *Causa*. Certainly such a man is dangerous to our cause."

"Don't the other waiters recognize him?"

"I think so. But no one has said anything. He is an old client."

"I am an old client too."

"Perhaps then he is on our side now, too."

"No," I said. "I know he is not."

"I have never denounced anyone."

"It is your problem. Maybe one of the other waiters will denounce him."

"No. Only the old waiters know him and the old waiters do not denounce."

"Bring another of the yellow gins and some bitters," I said. "There is tonic water still in the bottle."

"What's he talk about?" asked John. "I only understand little bit."

"There is a man here that we both knew in the old days. He used to be a marvelous pigeon shot and I used to see him at shoots. He is a fascist and for him to come here now, no matter what his reasons, is very foolish. But he was always very brave and very foolish."

"Show him to me."

"There at that table with the flyers."

"Which one?"

"With the very brown face; the cap over one eye. Who is laughing now."

"He is fascist?"

"Yes."

"That's a closest I see fascist since Fuentes del Ebro. Is a many fascist here?"

"Quite a few from time to time."

"Is drink the same drink as you," said John. "We drink that other people think we fascists, eh? Listen you ever been South America, West Coast, Magallanes?"

"No."

"Is all right. Only too many oc-toe-pus."

"Too many what?"

"Oc-toe-pus." He pronounced it with the accent on the toe as oc-*toe*-pus. "You know with the eight arms."

"Oh," I said. "Octopus."

"Oc-*toe*-pus," said John. "You see I am diver too. Is a good place to work all right make plenty money only too many oc-*toe*-pus."

"Did they bother you?"

"I don't know about that. First time I go down in Magallanes harbor I see oc-*toe*-pus. He is stand on his feet like this." John pointed his fingers on the table and brought his hands up, at the same time bringing up his shoulders and raising his eyebrows. "He is stand up taller than I am and he is look me right in the eye. I jerk cord for them to bring me up."

"How big was he, John?"

"I cannot say absolutely because the glass in the helmet make distort a little. But the head was big around more than four feet any*way*. And he was stand on his feet like on *tip*-toes and look at me like this. (He peered in my face.) So when I get up out of water they take off the helmet and so I say I don't go down there any more. Then the man of the job says, 'What a matter with you John? The oc-toe-pus is more afraid of you than you afraid of oc-toe-pus.' So I say to him 'Impossible!' What you say we drink some more this fascist drink?"

"All right," I said.

I was watching the man at the table. His name was Luis Delgado and the last time I had seen him had been in 1933 shooting pigeons at Saint Sebastian and I remembered standing with him up on top of the stand watching the final of the big shoot. We had a bet, more than I could afford to bet, and I believed a good deal more than he could afford to lose that year, and when he paid coming down the stairs, I remembered how pleasant he was and how he made it seem a great privilege to pay. Then I remembered our standing at the bar having a Martini, and I had that wonderful inner feeling of relief that comes when you have bet yourself out of a bad hole and I was wondering how badly the bet had hit him. I had shot rottenly all week and he had shot beautifully but drawn almost impossible birds and he had bet on himself steadily.

"Should we match a *duro?*" he asked.

"You really want to?"

"Yes, if you like."

"For how much?"

He took out a notecase and looked in it and laughed.

"I'd say for anything you like," he said. "But suppose we say for eight thousand pesetas. That's what seems to be there."

That was close to a thousand dollars then.

"Good," I said, all the fine inner quiet gone now and the hollow that gambling makes come back again. "Who's matching who?"

"I'll match you."

We shook the heavy silver five-peseta pieces in our cupped hands; then each man laid his coin on the back of his left hand, each coin covered with the right hand.

"What's yours?" he asked.

I uncovered the big silver piece with the profile of Alfonso XIII as a baby showing.

"Heads," I said.

"Take these damned things and be a good man and buy me a

drink," he emptied out the notecase. "You wouldn't like to buy a good Purdey gun would you?"

"No," I said. "But look, Luis, if you need some money—"

I was holding the stiffly folded, shiny-heavy-paper, green thousand-peseta notes toward him.

"Don't be silly, Enrique," he said. "We've been gambling, haven't we?"

└ Henry

"Yes. But we know each other quite well."

"Not that well."

"Right," I said. "You're the judge of that. Then what will you drink?"

"What about a gin and tonic? That's a marvelous drink you know."

So we had a gin and tonic and I felt very badly to have broken him and I felt awfully good to have won the money, and a gin and tonic never tasted better to me in all my life. There is no use to lie about these things or pretend you do not enjoy winning; but this boy Luis Delgado was a very pretty gambler.

"I don't think if people gambled for what they could afford it would be very interesting. Do you Enrique?"

"I don't know. I've never been able to afford it."

"Don't be silly. You have lots of money."

"No I haven't," I said. "Really."

"Oh everyone has money," he said. "It's just a question of selling something or other to get hold of it."

"I don't have much. Really."

"Oh don't be silly. I've never known an American who wasn't rich."

I guess that was the truth all right. He wouldn't have met them at the Ritz bar or at Chicote's either in those days. And now he was back in Chicote's and all the Americans he would meet there now were the kind he would never have met; except me, and I was a mistake. But I would have given plenty not to have seen him in there.

Still, if he wanted to do an absolutely damned fool thing like that it was his own business. But as I looked at the table and remembered the old days I felt badly about him and I felt very badly too that I had given the waiter the number of the counter-espionage bureau in Seguridad headquarters. He could have had

Seguridad by simply asking on the telephone. But I had given him the shortest cut to having Delgado arrested in one of those excesses of impartiality, righteousness and Pontius Pilatry, and the always-dirty desire to see how people act under an emotional conflict, that makes writers such attractive friends.

The waiter came over.

"What do you think?" he asked.

"I would never denounce him myself," I said, now trying to undo for myself what I had done with the number. "But I am a foreigner and it is your war and your problem."

"But you are with us."

"Absolutely and always. But it does not include denouncing old friends."

"But for me?"

"For you it is different."

I knew this was true and there was nothing else to say, only I wished I had never heard of any of it.

My curiosity as to how people would act in this case had been long ago, and shamefully, satisfied. I turned to John and did not look at the table where Luis Delgado was sitting. I knew he had been flying with the fascists for over a year, and here he was, in a loyalist uniform, talking to three young loyalist flyers of the last crop that had been trained in France.

None of those new kids would know him and I wondered whether he had come to try to steal a plane or for what. Whatever he was there for, he was a fool to come to Chicote's now.

"How do you feel, John?" I asked.

"Feel good," said John. "Is a good drink hokay. Makes me feel little bit drunk maybe. Is a good for the buzzing in the head."

The waiter came over. He was very excited.

"I have denounced him," he said.

"Well then," I said, "now you haven't any problem."

"No," he said proudly. "I have denounced him. They are on their way now to get him."

"Let's go," I said to John. "There is going to be some trouble here."

"Is best go then," said John. "Is a plenty trouble always come, even if you do best to avoid. How much we owe?"

"You aren't going to stay?" the waiter asked.

"No."

"But you gave me the telephone number."

"I know it. You get to know too many telephone numbers if you stay around in this town."

"But it was my duty."

"Yes. Why not? Duty is a very strong thing."

"But now?"

"Well, you felt good about it just now, didn't you? Maybe you will feel good about it again. Maybe you will get to like it."

"You have forgotten the package," the waiter said. He handed me the meat which was wrapped in two envelopes which had brought copies of the *Spur* to the piles of magazines which accumulated in one of the office rooms of the Embassy.

"I understand," I said to the waiter. "Truly."

"He was an old client and a good client. Also I have never denounced anyone before. I did not denounce for pleasure."

"Also I should not speak cynically or brutally. Tell him that I denounced him. He hates me anyway by now for differences in politics. He'd feel badly if he knew it was you."

"No. Each man must take his responsibility. But you understand?"

"Yes," I said. Then lied. "I understand and I approve." You have to lie very often in a war and when you have to lie you should do it quickly and as well as you can.

We shook hands and I went out the door with John. I looked back at the table where Luis Delgado sat as I went out. He had another gin and tonic in front of him and everyone at the table was laughing at something he had said. He had a very gay, brown face, and shooter's eyes, and I wondered what he was passing himself off as.

He was a fool to go to Chicote's. But that was exactly the sort of thing that he would do in order to be able to boast of it when he was back with his own people.

As we went out of the door and turned to walk up the street, a big Seguridad car drew up in front of Chicote's and eight men got out of it. Six with sub-machine guns took up positions outside the door. Two in plain clothes went inside. A man asked us for our papers and when I said, "Foreigners," he said to go along; that it was all right.

In the dark going up the Gran Via there was much new broken glass on the sidewalk and much rubble under foot from the shelling. The air was still smoky and all up the street it smelled of high explosive and blasted granite.

"Where you go eat?" asked John.

"I have some meat for all of us, and we can cook it in the room."

"I cook it," said John. "I cook good. I remember one time when I cook on ship—"

"It will be pretty tough," I said. "It's just been freshly butchered."

"Oh no," said John. "Is a no such thing as a tough meat in a war."

People were hurrying by in the dark on their way home from the cinemas where they had stayed until the shelling was over.

"What's a matter that fascist he come to that café where they know him?"

"He was crazy to do it."

"Is a trouble with a war," John said. "Is a too many people crazy."

"John," I said, "I think you've got something there."

Back at the hotel we went in the door past the sandbags piled to protect the porter's desk and I asked for the key, but the porter said there were two comrades upstairs in the room taking a bath. He had given them the keys.

"Go on up, John," I said. "I want to telephone."

I went over to the booth and called the same number I had given the waiter.

"Hello? Pepé?"

A thin-lipped voice came over the phone. "¿Qué tal Enrique?"

"Listen Pepé, did you pick up a certain Luis Delgado at Chicote's?"

"Si, hombre, si. Sin novedad. Without trouble."

"He doesn't know anything about the waiter?"

"No, hombre, no."

"Then don't tell him. Tell him I denounced him then, will you? Nothing about the waiter."

"Why when it will make no difference? He is a spy. He will be shot. There is no choice in the matter."

"I know," I said. "But it makes a difference."

"As you want, hombre. As you want. When shall I see thee?"

"Lunch tomorrow. We have some meat."

"And whiskey before. Good, hombre, good."

"Salud, Pepé, and thank you."

"Salud, Enrique. It is nothing. Salud."

It was a strange and very deadly voice and I never got used to hearing it, but as I walked up the stairs now, I felt much better.

All we old clients of Chicote's had a sort of feeling about the place. I knew that was why Luis Delgado had been such a fool as to go back there. He could have done his business some place else. But if he was in Madrid he had to go there. He had been a good client as the waiter had said and we had been friends. Certainly any small acts of kindness you can do in life are worth doing. So I was glad I had called my friend Pepé at Seguridad headquarters because Luis Delgado was an old client of Chicote's and I did not wish him to be disillusioned or bitter about the waiters there before he died.

Composed July–Sept. 1938
Pub. Esquire, Dec. 1938

The Butterfly and the Tank

2nd Chicote story

I.
A.
On this evening I was walking home from the censorship office *i.e., he is a war correspondent*
to the Florida Hotel and it was raining. So about halfway home
I got sick of the rain and stopped into Chicote's for a quick one.
It was the second winter of shelling in the siege of Madrid and
everything was short including tobacco and people's tempers and
you were a little hungry all the time and would become suddenly
and unreasonably irritated at things you could do nothing about
such as the weather. I should have gone on home. It was only five
blocks more, but when I saw Chicote's doorway I thought I
would get a quick one and then do those six blocks up the Gran
Via through the mud and rubble of the streets broken by the
bombardment.

The place was crowded. You couldn't get near the bar and all
the tables were full. It was full of smoke, singing, men in uniform, and the smell of wet leather coats, and they were handing
drinks over a crowd that was three deep at the bar.

A waiter I knew found a chair from another table and I sat
down with a thin, white-faced, Adam's-appled German I knew *German—*
who was working at the censorship and two other people I did *man—*
not know. The table was in the middle of the room a little on *woman—*
your right as you go in.

You couldn't hear yourself talk for the singing and I ordered a
gin and angostura and put it down against the rain. The place
was really packed and everybody was very jolly; maybe getting
just a little bit too jolly from the newly made Catalan liquor most
of them were drinking. A couple of people I did not know
slapped me on the back and when the girl at our table said something to me, I couldn't hear it and said, "Sure."

She was pretty terrible looking now I had stopped looking

101

around and was looking at our table; really pretty terrible. But it turned out, when the waiter came, that what she had asked me was to have a drink. The fellow with her was not very forceful looking but she was forceful enough for both of them. She had one of those strong, semi-classical faces and was built like a lion tamer; and the boy with her looked as though he ought to be wearing an old school tie. He wasn't though. He was wearing a leather coat just like all the rest of us. Only it wasn't wet because they had been there since before the rain started. She had on a leather coat too and it was becoming to the sort of face she had.

By this time I was wishing I had not stopped into Chicote's but had gone straight on home where you could change your clothes and be dry and have a drink in comfort on the bed with your feet up, and I was tired of looking at both of these young people. Life is very short and ugly women are very long and sitting there at the table I decided that even though I was a writer and supposed to have an insatiable curiosity about all sorts of people, I did not really care to know whether these two were married, or what they saw in each other, or what their politics were, or whether he had a little money, or she had a little money, or anything about them. I decided they must be in the radio. Any time you saw really strange looking civilians in Madrid they were always in the radio. So to say something I raised my voice above the noise and asked, "You in the radio?"

"We are," the girl said. So that was that. They were in the radio.

"How are you comrade?" I said to the German.

"Fine. And you?"

"Wet," I said, and he laughed with his head on one side.

"You haven't got a cigarette?" he asked. I handed him my next to the last pack of cigarettes and he took two. The forceful girl took two and the young man with the old school tie face took one.

"Take another," I shouted.

"No thanks," he answered and the German took it instead.

"Do you mind?" he smiled.

"Of course not," I said. I really minded and he knew it. But he wanted the cigarettes so badly that it did not matter. The singing had died down momentarily, or there was a break in it as there is sometimes in a storm, and we could all hear what we said.

"You been here long?" the forceful girl asked me. She pronounced it bean as in bean soup.

"Off and on," I said.

"We must have a serious talk," the German said. "I want to have a talk with you. When can we have it?"

"I'll call you up," I said. This German was a very strange German indeed and none of the good Germans liked him. He lived under the delusion that he could play the piano, but if you kept him away from pianos he was all right unless he was exposed to liquor, or the opportunity to gossip, and nobody had even been able to keep him away from those two things yet.

Gossip was the best thing he did and he always knew something new and highly discreditable about anyone you could mention in Madrid, Valencia, Barcelona, and other political centers.

Just then the singing really started in again, and you cannot gossip very well shouting, so it looked like a dull afternoon at Chicote's and I decided to leave as soon as I should have bought a round myself.

Just then it started. A civilian in a brown suit, a white shirt, black tie, his hair brushed straight back from a rather high forehead, who had been clowning around from table to table, squirted one of the waiters with a flit gun. Everybody laughed except the waiter who was carrying a tray full of drinks at the time. He was indignant.

"No hay derecho," the waiter said. This means, "You have no right to do that," and is the simplest and the strongest protest in Spain.

The flit gun man, delighted with his success, and not seeming to give any importance to the fact that it was well into the second year of the war, that he was in a city under siege where everyone was under a strain, and that he was one of only four men in civilian clothes in the place, now squirted another waiter.

I looked around for a place to duck to. This waiter, also, was indignant and the flit gun man squirted him twice more, lightheartedly. Some people still thought it was funny, including the forceful girl. But the waiter stood, shaking his head. His lips were trembling. He was an old man and he had worked in Chicote's for ten years that I knew of.

"No hay derecho," he said with dignity.

People had laughed, however, and the flit gun man, not noticing how the singing had fallen off, squirted his flit gun at the back of a waiter's neck. The waiter turned, holding his tray.

"No hay derecho," he said. This time it was no protest. It was an indictment and I saw three men in uniform start from a table for the flit gun man and the next thing all four of them were going out the revolving door in a rush and you heard a smack when someone hit the flit gun man on the mouth. Somebody else picked up the flit gun and threw it out the door after him.

The three men came back in looking serious, tough and very righteous. Then the door revolved and in came the flit gun man. His hair was down in his eyes, there was blood on his face, his necktie was pulled to one side and his shirt was torn open. He had the flit gun again and as he pushed, wild-eyed and white-faced, into the room he made one general, unaimed, challenging squirt with it, holding it toward the whole company.

I saw one of the three men start for him and I saw this man's face. There were more men with him now and they forced the flit gun man back between two tables on the left of the room as you go in, the flit gun man struggling wildly now, and when the shot went off I grabbed the forceful girl by the arm and dove for the kitchen door.

The kitchen door was shut and when I put my shoulder against it it did not give.

"Get down here behind the angle of the bar," I said. She knelt there.

"Flat," I said and pushed her down. She was furious.

Every man in the room except the German, who lay behind a table, and the public-school-looking boy who stood in a corner drawn up against the wall, had a gun out. On a bench along the wall three over-blonde girls, their hair dark at the roots, were standing on tiptoe to see and screaming steadily.

"I'm not afraid," the forceful one said. "This is ridiculous."

"You don't want to get shot in a café brawl," I said. "If that flit king has any friends here this can be very bad."

But he had no friends, evidently, because people began putting their pistols away and somebody lifted down the blonde screamers and everyone who had started over there when the shot came, drew back away from the flit man who lay, quietly, on his back on the floor.

"No one is to leave until the police come," someone shouted from the door.

Two policemen with rifles, who had come in off the street patrol, were standing by the door and at this announcement I saw six men form up just like the line-up of a football team coming out of a huddle and head out through the door. Three of them were the men who had first thrown the flit king out. One of them was the man who shot him. They went right through the policemen with the rifles like good interference taking out an end and a tackle. And as they went out one of the policemen got his rifle across the door and shouted, "No one can leave. Absolutely no one."

"Why did those men go? Why hold us if anyone's gone?"

"They were mechanics who had to return to their air field," someone said.

"But if anyone's gone it's silly to hold the others."

"Everyone must wait for the Seguridad. Things must be done legally and in order."

"But don't you see that if any person has gone it is silly to hold the others?"

"No one can leave. Everyone must wait."

"It's comic," I said to the forceful girl.

"No it's not. It's simply horrible."

We were standing up now and she was staring indignantly at where the flit king was lying. His arms were spread wide and he had one leg drawn up.

"I'm going over to help that poor wounded man. Why has no one helped him or done anything for him?"

"I'd leave him alone," I said. "You want to keep out of this."

"But it's simply inhuman. I've nurse's training and I'm going to give him first aid."

"I wouldn't," I said. "Don't go near him."

"Why not?" She was very upset and almost hysterical.

"Because he's dead," I said.

When the police came they held everybody there for three hours. They commenced by smelling of all the pistols. In this manner they would detect one which had been fired recently.

After about forty pistols they seemed to get bored with this and anyway all you could smell was wet leather coats. Then they sat at a table placed directly behind the late flit king, who lay on the floor looking like a grey wax caricature of himself, with grey wax hands and a grey wax face, and examined people's papers.

With his shirt ripped open you could see the flit king had no undershirt and the soles of his shoes were worn through. He looked very small and pitiful lying there on the floor. You had to step over him to get to the table where two plain clothes police-men sat and examined everyone's identification papers. The hus-band lost and found his papers several times with nervousness. He had a safe conduct pass somewhere but he had mislaid it in a pocket but he kept on searching and perspiring until he found it. Then he would put it in a different pocket and have to go searching again. He perspired heavily while doing this and it made his hair very curly and his face red. He now looked as though he should have not only an old school tie but one of those little caps boys in the lower forms wear. You have heard how events age people. Well this shooting had made him look about ten years younger.

While we were waiting around I told the forceful girl I thought the whole thing was a pretty good story and that I would write it sometime. The way the six had lined up in single file and rushed that door was very impressive. She was shocked and said that I could not write it because it would be prejudicial to the cause of the Spanish Republic. I said that I had been in Spain for a long time and that they used to have a phenomenal number of shootings in the old days around Valencia under the monarchy, and that for hundreds of years before the Republic people had been cutting each other with large knives called Navajas in Andalucia, and that if I saw a comic shooting in Chicote's during the war I could write about it just as though it had been in New York, Chicago, Key West or Marseilles. It did not have anything to do with politics. She said I shouldn't. Probably a lot of other people will say I shouldn't too. The German seemed to think it was a pretty good story however, and I gave him the last of the Camels. Well, anyway, finally, after about three hours the police said we could go.

They were sort of worried about me at the Florida because in those days, with the shelling, if you started for home on foot and

Next Day

didn't get there after the bars were closed at seven-thirty, people worried. I was glad to get home and I told the story while we were cooking supper on an electric stove and it had quite a success.

Well, it stopped raining during the night, and the next morning it was a fine, bright, cold early winter day and at twelve forty-five I pushed open the revolving doors at Chicote's to try a little gin and tonic before lunch. There were very few people there at that hour and two waiters and the manager came over to the table. They were all smiling.

"Did they catch the murderer?" I asked.

"Don't make jokes so early in the day," the manager said. "Did *you* see him shot?"

"Yes," I told him.

"Me too," he said. "I was just here when it happened." He pointed to a corner table. "He placed the pistol right against the man's chest when he fired."

"How late did they hold people?"

"Oh until past two this morning."

"They only came for the *fiambre*," using the Spanish slang word for corpse, the same used on menus for cold meat, "at eleven o'clock this morning."

"But you don't know about it yet," the manager said.

"No. He doesn't know," a waiter said.

"It is a very rare thing," another waiter said. "*Muy raro.*"

"And sad too," the manager said. He shook his head.

"Yes. Sad and curious," the waiter said. "Very sad."

"Tell me."

"It is a very rare thing," the manager said.

"Tell me. Come on tell me."

The manager leaned over the table in great confidence.

"In the flit gun, you know," he said. "He had *eau de cologne*. Poor fellow."

"It was not a joke in such bad taste, you see?" the waiter said.

"It was really just gaiety. No one should have taken offense," the manager said. "Poor fellow."

"I see," I said. "He just wanted everyone to have a good time."

"Yes," said the manager. "It was really just an unfortunate misunderstanding."

"And what about the flit gun?"

"The police took it. They have sent it around to his family."

"I imagine they will be glad to have it," I said.

"Yes," said the manager. "Certainly. A flit gun is always useful."

"Who was he?"

"A cabinet maker."

"Married?"

"Yes the wife was here with the police this morning."

"What did she say?"

"She dropped down by him and said, 'Pedro, what have they done to thee, Pedro? Who has done this to thee? Oh Pedro.'"

"Then the police had to take her away because she could not control herself," the waiter said.

"It seems he was feeble of the chest," the manager said. "He fought in the first days of the movement. They said he fought in the Sierra but he was too weak in the chest to continue."

"And yesterday afternoon he just went out on the town to cheer things up," I suggested.

"No," said the manager. "You see it is very rare. Everything is *muy raro*. This I learn from the police who are very efficient if given time. They have interrogated comrades from the shop where he worked. This they located from the card of his syndicate which was in his pocket. Yesterday he bought the flit gun and *agua de colonia* to use for a joke at a wedding. He had announced this intention. He bought them across the street. There was a label on the cologne bottle with the address. The bottle was in the washroom. It was there he filled the flit gun. After buying them he must have come in here when the rain started."

"I remember when he came in," a waiter said.

"In the gaiety, with the singing, he became gay too."

"He was gay all right," I said. "He was practically floating around."

The manager kept on with the relentless Spanish logic.

"That is the gaiety of drinking with a weakness of the chest," he said.

"I don't like this story very well," I said.

"Listen," said the manager. "How rare it is. His gaiety comes in contact with the seriousness of the war like a butterfly—"

"Oh very like a butterfly," I said. "Too much like a butterfly."

"I am not joking," said the manager. "You see it? Like a butterfly and a tank."

This pleased him enormously. He was getting into the real Spanish metaphysics.

"Have a drink on the house," he said. "You must write a story about this."

I remembered the flit gun man with his gray wax hands and his grey wax face, his arms spread wide and his legs drawn up and he did look a little like a butterfly; not too much, you know. But he did not look very human either. He reminded me more of a dead sparrow.

"I'll take gin and Schweppes quinine tonic water," I said.

"You must write a story about it," the manager said. "Here. Here's luck."

"Luck," I said. "Look, an English girl last night told me I shouldn't write about it. That it would be very bad for the cause."

"What nonsense," the manager said. "It is very interesting and important, the misunderstood gaiety coming in contact with the deadly seriousness that is here always. To me it is the rarest and most interesting thing which I have seen for some time. You must write it."

"All right," I said. "Sure. Has he any children?"

"No," he said. "I asked the police. But you must write it and you must call it The Butterfly and the Tank."

"All right," I said. "Sure. But I don't like the title much."

"The title is very elegant," the manager said. "It is pure literature."

"All right," I said. "Sure. That's what we'll call it. The Butterfly and the Tank."

And I sat there on that bright cheerful morning, the place smelling clean and newly aired and swept, with the manager who was an old friend and who was now very pleased with the literature we were making together and I took a sip of the gin and tonic water and looked out the sandbagged window and thought of the wife kneeling there and saying, "Pedro. *Pedro*, who has done this to thee, Pedro?" And I thought that the police would never be able to tell her that even if they had the name of the man who pulled the trigger.

Composed Sept. - Oct. 1938
Pub. Esquire, Feb. 1939

Night Before Battle 3rd Chicote Story

Narrator = Harry Emmunds

I. At this time we were working in a shell smashed house that overlooked the Casa del Campo in Madrid. Below us a battle was being fought. You could see it spread out below you and over the hills, could smell it, could taste the dust of it, and the noise of it was one great slithering sheet of rifle and automatic rifle fire rising and dropping, and in it came the crack of the guns and the bubbly rumbling of the outgoing shells fired from the batteries behind us, the thud of their bursts, and then the rolling yellow clouds of dust. But it was just too far to film well. We had tried working closer but they kept sniping at the camera and you could not work.

The big camera was the most expensive thing we had and if it was smashed we were through. We were making the film on almost nothing and all the money was in the cans of film and the cameras. We could not afford to waste film and you had to be awfully careful of the cameras.

The day before we had been sniped out of a good place to film from and I had to crawl back holding the small camera to my belly, trying to keep my head lower than my shoulders, hitching along on my elbows, the bullets whocking into the brick wall over my back and twice spurting dirt over me.

Our heaviest attacks were made in the afternoon, God knows why, as the fascists then had the sun at their backs, and it shone on the camera lenses and made them blink like a helio and the Moors would open up on the flash. They knew all about helios and officers' glasses, from the Riff and if you wanted to be properly sniped, all you had to do was use a pair of glasses without shading them adequately. They could shoot too, and they had kept my mouth dry all day.

110

In the afternoon we moved up into the house. It was a fine place to work and we made a sort of a blind for the camera on a balcony with the broken latticed curtains; but, as I said, it was too far.

It was not too far to get the pine studded hillside, the lake and the outline of the stone farm buildings that disappeared in the sudden smashes of stone dust from the hits by high explosive shells, nor was it too far to get the clouds of smoke and dirt that thundered up on the hill crest as the bombers droned over. But at eight hundred to a thousand yards the tanks looked like small mud-colored beetles bustling in the trees and spitting tiny flashes and the men behind them were toy men who lay flat, then crouched and ran, and then dropped to run again, or to stay where they lay, spotting the hillside as the tanks moved on. Still we hoped to get the shape of the battle. We had many close shots and would get others with luck and if we could get the sudden fountainings of earth, the puffs of shrapnel, the rolling clouds of smoke and dust lit by the yellow flash and white blossoming of grenades that is the very shape of battle we would have something that we needed.

So when the light failed we carried the big camera down the stairs, took off the tripod, made three loads, and then one at a time, sprinted across the fire-swept corner of the Paseo Rosales into the lee of the stone wall of the stables of the old Montana Barracks. We knew we had a good place to work and we felt cheerful. But we were kidding ourselves plenty that it was not too far.

"Come on let's go to Chicote's," I said when we had come up the hill to the Hotel Florida.

But they had to repair a camera, to change film and seal up what we had made so I went alone. You were never alone in Spain and it felt good for a change.

As I started to walk down the Gran Via to Chicote's in the April twilight I felt happy, cheerful and excited. We had worked hard, and I thought well. But walking down the street alone, all my elation died. Now that I was alone and there was no excitement, I knew we had been too far away and any fool could see the offensive was a failure. I had known it all day but you are often deceived by hope and optimism. But remembering how it looked now, I knew this was just another blood bath like the Somme. The people's army was on the offensive finally. But it was attacking in a way that could do only one thing: destroy itself. And as I put together now what I had seen all day and what I had heard, I felt plenty bad.

I knew in the smoke and din of Chicote's that the offensive was a failure and I knew it even stronger when I took my first drink at the crowded bar. When things are all right and it is you that is feeling low a drink can make you feel better. But when things are really bad and you are all right, a drink just makes it clearer. Now, in Chicote's it was so crowded that you had to make room with your elbows to get your drink to your mouth. I had one good long swallow and then someone jostled me so that I spilled part of the glass of whisky and soda. I looked around angrily and the man who had jostled me laughed.

"Hello fish face," he said.

"Hello you goat."

"Let's get a table," he said. "You certainly looked sore when I bumped you."

"Where did you come from?" I asked. His leather coat was dirty and greasy, his eyes were hollow and he needed a shave. He had the big Colt automatic that had belonged to three other men that I had known of, and that we were always trying to get shells for, strapped to his leg. He was very tall and his face was smoke darkened and grease smudged. He had a leather helmet with a heavy leather padded ridge longitudinally over the top and a heavily padded leather rim.

"Where'd you come from?"

"Casa del Campo," he said, pronouncing it in a sing-song mocking way we had heard a page boy use in calling in the lobby of a hotel in New Orleans one time and still kept as a private joke.

"There's a table," I said as two soldiers and two girls got up to go. "Let's get it."

We sat at this table in the middle of the room and I watched him raise his glass. His hands were greasy and the forks of both thumbs black as graphite from the back spit of the machine gun. The hand holding the drink was shaking.

"Look at them," he put out the other hand. It was shaking too. "Both the same," he said in that same comic lilt. Then, seriously, "You been down there?"

"We're making a picture of it."

"Photograph well?"

"Not too."

"See us?"

"Where?"

"Attack on the farm. Three twenty-five this afternoon."

"Oh, yes."

"Like it?"

"Nope."

"Me either," he said. "Listen the whole thing is just as crazy as a bedbug. Why do they want to make a frontal attack against positions like those? Who in hell thought it up?"

"An S. O. B. named Largo Caballero," said a short man with thick glasses who was sitting at the table when we came over to it. "The first time they let him look through a pair of field glasses he became a general. This is his masterpiece."

We both looked at the man who spoke. Al Wagner, the tank man, looked at me and raised what had been his eyebrows before they were burnt off. The little man smiled at us.

"If anyone around here speaks English you're liable to get shot Comrade," Al said to him.

"No," said the little short man. "Largo Caballero is liable to be shot. He ought to be shot."

"Listen Comrade," said Al. "Just speak a little quieter will you? Somebody might overhear you and think we were with you."

"I know what I'm talking about," said the short man with the very thick glasses. I looked at him carefully. He gave you a certain feeling that he did.

"Just the same it isn't always a good thing to say what you know," I said. "Have a drink?"

"Certainly," he said. "It's all right to talk to you. I know you. You're all right."

"I'm not *that* all right," I said. "And this is a public bar."

"A public bar is the only private place there is. Nobody can hear what we say here. What is your unit, Comrade?"

"I've got some tanks about eight minutes from here on foot,"
Al told him. "We are through for the day and I have the early
part of this evening off."

"Why don't you ever get washed?" I said.

"I plan to," said Al. "In your room. When we leave here. Have
you got any mechanic's soap?"

"No."

"That's all right," he said. "I've got a little here with me in my
pocket that I've been saving."

The little man with the thick lensed glasses was looking at
Al intently.

"Are you a party member, Comrade?" he asked.

"Sure," said Al.

"I know Comrade Henry here is not," the little man said.

"I wouldn't trust him then," Al said. "I never do."

"You bastid," I said. "Want to go?"

"No," Al said. "I need another drink very badly."

"I know all about Comrade Henry," the little man said. "Now
let me tell you something more about Largo Caballero."

"Do we have to hear it?" Al asked. "Remember I'm in the
people's army. You don't think it will discourage me do you?"

"You know his head is swelled so badly now he's getting sort
of mad. He is Prime Minister and War Minister and nobody can
even talk to him anymore. You know he's just a good honest
trade union leader somewhere between the late Sam Gompers
and John L. Lewis but this man Araquistain who invented him?"

"Take it easy," said Al. "I don't follow."

"Oh Araquistain invented him. Araquistain who is Ambassa-
dor in Paris now. He made him up you know. He called him
the Spanish Lenin and then the poor man tried to live up to it
and somebody let him look through a pair of field glasses and he
thought he was Clausewitz."

"You said that before," Al told him coldly. "What do you base
it on?"

"Why three days ago in the Cabinet meeting he was talking
military affairs. They were talking about this business we've
got now and Jesus Hernandez, just ribbing him you know, asked
him what was the difference between tactics and strategy. Do
you know what the old boy said?"

"No," Al said. I could see this new Comrade was getting a little on his nerves.

"He said, 'In tactics you attack the enemy from in front. In strategy you take him from the sides.' Now isn't that something?"

"You better run along, Comrade," Al said. "You're getting so awfully discouraged."

"But we'll get rid of Largo Caballero," the short Comrade said. "We'll get rid of him right after his offensive. This last piece of stupidity will be the end of him."

"O.K. Comrade," Al told him. "But I've got to attack in the morning."

"Oh you are going to attack again?"

"Listen Comrade. You can tell me any sort of crap you want because it's interesting and I'm grown up enough to sort things out. But don't ask me any questions, see? Because you'll be in trouble."

"I just meant it personally. Not as information."

"We don't know each other well enough to ask personal questions, Comrade," Al said. "Why don't you just go to another table and let Comrade Henry and me talk. I want to ask him some things."

"Salud Comrade," the little man said, standing up. "We'll meet another time."

"Good," said Al. "Another time."

We watched him go over to another table. He excused himself, some soldiers made room for him, and as we watched we could see him starting to talk. They all looked interested.

"What do you make of that little guy?" Al asked.

"I don't know."

"Me either," Al said. "He certainly had this offensive sized up." He took a drink and showed his hand. "See? It's all right now. I'm not any rummy either. I never take a drink before an attack."

"How was it today?"

"You saw it. How did it look?"

"Terrible."

"That's it. That's the word for it all right. It was terrible. I guess he's using strategy and tactics both now because we are attacking from straight in front and from both sides. How's the rest of it going?"

"Duran took the new race track. The *hipódromo*. We've narrowed down on the corridor that runs up into University City. Up above we crossed the Coruña road. And we're stopped at the Cerro de Aguilar since yesterday morning. We were up that way this morning. Duran lost over half his brigade, I heard. How is it with you?"

"Tomorrow we're going to try those farm houses and the church again. The church on the hill, the one they call the hermit, is the objective. The whole hillside is cut by those gullies and it's all enfiladed at least three ways by machine gun posts. They're dug deep all through there and it's well done. We haven't got enough artillery to give any kind of real covering fire to keep them down and we haven't heavy artillery to blow them out. They've got anti-tanks in those three houses and an anti-tank battery by the church. It's going to be murder."

"When's it for?"

"Don't ask me. I've got no right to tell you that."

"If we have to film it, I meant," I said. "The money from the film all goes for ambulances. We've got the Twelfth Brigade in the counter-attack at the Arganda Bridge. And we've got the Twelfth again in that attack last week by Pingarrón. We got some good tank shots there." <small>(A writ - the International Brigade</small>

"The tanks were no good there," Al said.

"I know," I said, "but they photographed very well. What about tomorrow?"

"Just get out early and wait," he said. "Not too early."

"How you feel now?"

"I'm awfully tired," he said. "And I've got a bad headache. But I feel a lot better. Let's have another one and then go up to your place and get a bath."

"Maybe we ought to eat first."

"I'm too dirty to eat. You can hold a place and I'll go get a bath and join you at the Gran Via."

"I'll go up with you."

"No. It's better to hold a place and I'll join you." He leaned his head forward on the table. "Boy I got a headache. It's the noise in those buckets. I never hear it any more but it does something to your ears just the same."

"Why don't you go to bed?"

"No. I'd rather stay up with you for a while and then sleep when I get back down there. I don't want to wake up twice."

"You haven't got the horrors, have you?"

"No," he said. "I'm fine. Listen, Hank. I don't want to talk a lot of crap but I think I'm going to get killed tomorrow."

I touched the table three times with my finger tips.

"Everybody feels like that. I've felt like that plenty of times."

"No," he said. "It's not natural with me. But where we've got to go tomorrow doesn't make sense. I don't even know that I can get them up there. You can't make them move if they won't go. You can shoot them afterwards. But at the time if they won't go they won't go. If you shoot them they still won't go."

"Maybe it will be all right."

"No. We've got good infantry tomorrow. They'll go anyway. Not like those yellow bastids we had the first day."

"Maybe it will be all right."

"No," he said. "It won't be all right. But it will be just exactly as good as I can make it. I can make them start all right and I can take them up to where they will have to quit one at a time. Maybe they can make it. I've got three I can rely on. If only one of the good ones doesn't get knocked out at the start."

"Who are your good ones?"

"I've got a big Greek from Chicago that will go anywhere. He's just as good as they come. I've got a Frenchman from Marseille that's got his left shoulder in a cast with two wounds still draining that asked to come out of the hospital in the Palace Hotel for this show and has to be strapped in and I don't know how he can do it. Just technically I mean. He'd break your bloody heart. He used to be a taxi driver." He stopped. "I'm talking too much. Stop me if I talk too much."

"Who's the third one?" I asked.

"The third one? Did I say I had a third one?"

"Sure."

"Oh yes," he said. "That's me."

"What about the others?"

"They're mechanics, but they couldn't learn to soldier. They can't size up what's happening. And they're all afraid to die. I tried to get them over it," he said. "But it comes back on them every attack. They look like tank men when you see them by the tanks with the helmets on. They look like tank men when they get in. But when they shut the traps down there's really nothing inside. They aren't tank men. And so far we haven't had time to make new ones."

"Do you want to take the bath?"

"Let's sit here a little while longer," he said. "It's nice here."

"It's funny all right, with a war right down the end of the street so you can walk to it, and then leave it and come here."

"And then walk back to it," Al said.

"What about a girl? There's two American girls at the Florida. Newspaper correspondents. Maybe you could make one."

"I don't want to have to talk to them. I'm too tired."

"There's the two Moor girls from Ceuta at that corner table."

He looked over at them. They were both dark and bushy headed. One was large and one was small and they certainly both looked strong and active.

"No," said Al. "I'm going to see plenty Moors tomorrow without having to fool with them tonight."

"There's plenty of girls," I said. "Manolita's at the Florida. That Seguridad bird she lives with has gone to Valencia and she's being true to him with everybody."

"Listen, Hank, what are you trying to promote me?"

"I just wanted to cheer you up."

"Grow up," he said. "What's one more?"

"One more."

"I don't mind dying a bit," he said. "Dying is just a lot of crap. Only it's wasteful. The attack is wrong and it's wasteful. I can handle tanks good now. If I had time I could make good tankists too. And if we had tanks that were a little bit faster the anti-tanks wouldn't bother them the way it does when you haven't got the mobility. Listen, Hank, they aren't what we thought they were though. Do you remember when everybody thought if we only had tanks?"

"They were good at Guadalajara."

"Sure. But those were the old boys. They were soldiers. And it was against Italians."

"But what's happened?"

"A lot of things. The mercenaries signed up for six months. Most of them were Frenchmen. They soldiered good for five but now all they want to do is live through the last month and go home. They aren't worth a damn now. The Russians that came out as demonstrators when the government bought the tanks were perfect. But they're pulling them back now for China they say. The new Spaniards are some of them good and some not. It takes six months to make a good tank man, I mean to know anything. And be able to size up and work intelligently you have to have a talent. We've been having to make them in six weeks and there aren't so many with a talent."

"They make fine flyers."

"They'll make fine tank guys too. But you have to get the ones with a vocation for it. It's sort of like being a priest. You have to be cut out for it. Especially now they've got so much anti-tank."

They had pulled down the shutters in Chicote's and now they were locking the door. No one would be allowed in now. But you had a half an hour more before they closed.

"I like it here," said Al. "It isn't so noisy now. Remember that time I met you in New Orleans when I was on a ship and we went in to have a drink in the Monteleone bar and that kid that looked just like Saint Sebastian was paging people with that funny voice like he was singing and I gave him a quarter to page Mr. B. F. Slob?"

"That's the same way you said 'Casa del Campo.'"

"Yeah," he said. "I laugh every time I think of that." Then he went on, "You see, now, they're not frightened of tanks anymore. Nobody is. We aren't either. But they're still useful. Really useful. Only with the anti-tank now they're so damn vulnerable. Maybe I ought to be in something else. *Not really.* Because they're still useful. But the way they are now you've got to have a vocation for them. You got to have a lot of political development to be a good tank man now."

"You're a good tank man."

"I'd like to be something else tomorrow," he said. "I'm talking awfully wet but you have a right to talk wet if it isn't going to hurt anybody else. You know I like tanks too, only we don't use them right because the infantry don't know enough yet. They just want the old tank ahead to give them some cover while they go. That's no good. Then they get to depending on the tanks and they won't move without them. Sometimes they won't even deploy."

"I know."

"But you see if you had tankists that knew their stuff they'd go out ahead and develop the machine gun fire and then drop back behind the infantry and fire on the gun and knock it out and give the infantry covering fire when they attacked. And other tanks could rush the machine gun posts as though they were cavalry. And they could straddle a trench and enfilade and put flanking fire down it. And they could bring up infantry when it was right to or cover their advance when that was best."

"But instead?"

"Instead it's like it will be tomorrow. We have so damned few guns that we're just used as slightly mobile armored artillery units. And as soon as you are standing still and being light artillery, you've lost your mobility and that's your safety and they start sniping at you with the anti-tanks. And if we're not that we're just sort of iron perambulators to push ahead of the infantry. And lately you don't know whether the perambulator will push or whether the guys inside will push them. And you never know if there's going to be anybody behind you when you get there."

"How many are you now to a brigade?"

"Six to a battalion. Thirty to a brigade. That's in principle."

"Why don't you come along now and get the bath and we'll go and eat?"

"All right. But don't you start taking care of me or thinking I'm worried or anything because I'm not. I'm just tired and I wanted to talk. And don't give me any pep talk either because we've got a political commissar and I know what I'm fighting for and I'm not worried. But I'd like things to be efficient and used as intelligently as possible."

"What made you think I was going to give you any pep talk?"

"You started to look like it."

"All I tried to do was see if you wanted a girl and not to talk too wet about getting killed."

"Well I don't want any girl tonight and I'll talk just as wet as I please unless it does damage to others. Does it damage you?"

"Come on and get the bath," I said. "You can talk just as bloody wet as you want."

"Who do you suppose that little guy was that talked as though he knew so much?"

"I don't know," I said. "But I'm going to find out."

"He made me gloomy," said Al. "Come on. Let's go."

The old waiter with the bald head unlocked the outside door of Chicote's and let us out into the street.

"How is the offensive, Comrades?" he said at the door.

"It's O. K., Comrade," said Al. "It's all right."

"I am happy," said the waiter. "My boy is in the One Hundred and Forty-fifth Brigade. Have you seen them?"

"I am of the tanks," said Al. "This Comrade makes a cinema. Have you seen the hundred and forty-fifth?"

"No," I said.

"They are up the Extremadura road," the old waiter said. "My boy is political commissar of the machine gun company of his battalion. He is my youngest boy. He is twenty."

"What party are you Comrade?" Al asked him.

"I am of no party," the waiter said. "But my boy is a Communist."

"So am I," said Al. "The offensive, Comrade, has not yet reached a decision. It is very difficult. The fascists hold very strong positions. You, in the rear-guard, must be as firm as we will be at the front. We may not take these positions now but we have proved we now have an army capable of going on the offensive and you will see what it will do."

"And the Extremadura road?" asked the old waiter, still holding to the door. "Is it very dangerous there?"

"No," said Al. "It's fine up there. You don't need to worry about him up there."

"God bless you," said the waiter. "God guard you and keep you."

Outside in the dark street, Al said, "Jees he's kind of confused politically, isn't he?"

"He is a good guy," I said. "I've known him for a long time."

"He seems like a good guy," Al said. "But he ought to get wise to himself politically."

II. The room at the Florida was crowded. They were playing the gramophone and it was full of smoke and there was a crap game going on the floor. Comrades kept coming in to use the bathtub and the room smelt of smoke, soap, dirty uniforms, and steam from the bathroom.

The Spanish girl called Manolita, very neat, demurely dressed, with a sort of false French chic, with much joviality, much dignity and closely set cold eyes, was sitting on the bed talking with an English newspaper man. Except for the gramophone it wasn't very noisy.

"It *is* your room isn't it?" the English newspaper man said.

"It's in my name at the desk," I said. "I sleep in it sometimes."

"But whose is the whisky?" he asked.

"Mine," said Manolita. "They drank that bottle so I got another."

"You're a good girl, daughter," I said. "That's three I owe you."

"Two," she said. "The other was a present."

There was a huge cooked ham, rosy and white edged in a half opened tin on the table beside my typewriter and a comrade would reach up, cut himself a slice of ham with his pocket knife, and go back to the crap game. I cut myself a slice of ham.

"You're next on the tub," I said to Al. He had been looking around the room.

"It's nice here," he said. "Where did the ham come from?"

"We bought it from the *Intendencia* of one of the brigades," she said. "Isn't it beautiful?"

"Who's we?"

"He and I," she said, turning her head toward the English correspondent. "Don't you think he's cute?"

"Manolita has been most kind," said the Englishman. "I hope we're not disturbing you."

"Not at all," I said. "Later on I might want to use the bed but that won't be until much later."

"We can have a party in my room," Manolita said. "You aren't cross are you, Henry?"

"Never," I said. "Who are the Comrades shooting craps?"

"I don't know," said Manolita. "They came in for baths and then they stayed to shoot craps. Everyone has been very nice. You know my bad news?"

"No."

"It's very bad. You knew my fiancé who was in the police and went to Barcelona?"

"Yes. Sure."

Al went into the bathroom.

"Well he was shot in an accident and I haven't any one I can depend on in police circles and he never got me the papers he had promised me and today I heard I was going to be arrested."

"Why?"

"Because I have no papers and they say I hang around with you people and with people from the Brigades all the time so I am probably a spy. If my fiancé had not gotten himself shot it would have been all right. Will you help me?"

"Sure," I said. "Nothing will happen to you if you're all right."

"I think I'd better stay with you to be sure."

"And if you're not all right that would be fine for me wouldn't it?"

"Can't I stay with you?"

"No. If you get in trouble call me up. I never heard you ask anybody any military questions. I think you're all right."

"I'm *really* all right," she said then, leaning over, away from the Englishman. "You think it's all right to stay with him? Is *he* all right?"

"How do I know?" I said. "I never saw him before."

"You're being cross," she said. "Let's not think about it now but everyone be happy and go out to dinner."

I went over to the crap game.

"You want to go out to dinner?"

"No, Comrade," said the man handling the dice without looking up. "You want to get in the game?"

"I want to eat."

"We'll be here when you get back," said another crap shooter. "Come on, roll, I've got you covered."

"If you run into any money bring it up here to the game."

There was one in the room I knew beside Manolita. He was from the Twelfth Brigade and he was playing the gramophone.

He was a Hungarian, a sad Hungarian, not one of the cheerful kind.

"Salud Camarade," he said. "Thank you for your hospitality."

"Don't you shoot craps?" I asked him.

"I haven't that sort of money," he said. "They are aviators with contracts. Mercenaries . . . They make a thousand dollars a month. They were on the Teruel front and now they have come here."

"How did they come up here?"

"One of them knows you. But he had to go out to his field. They came for him in a car and the game had already started."

"I'm glad you came up," I said. "Come up any time and make yourself at home."

"I came to play the new discs," he said. "It does not disturb you?"

"No. It's fine. Have a drink."

"A little ham," he said.

One of the crap shooters reached up and cut a slice of ham.

"You haven't seen this guy Henry around that owns the place, have you?" he asked me.

"That's me."

"Oh," he said. "Sorry. Want to get in the game?"

"Later on," I said.

"O.K.," he said. Then his mouth full of ham, "Listen you tar heel bastid. Make your dice hit the wall and bounce."

"Won't make no difference to you, Comrade," said the man handling the dice.

Al came out of the bathroom. He looked all clean except for some smudges around his eyes.

"You can take those off with a towel," I said.

"What?"

"Look at yourself once more in the mirror."

"It's too steamy," he said. "To hell with it, I feel clean."

"Let's eat," I said. "Come on Manolita. You know each other?"

I watched her eyes run over Al.

"How are you?" Manolita said.

"I say that is a sound idea," the Englishman said. "Do let's eat. But where?"

"Is that a crap game?" Al said.

"Didn't you see it when you came in?"

"No," he said. "All I saw was the ham."

"It's a crap game."

"You go and eat," Al said. "I'm staying here."

As we went out there were six of them on the floor and Al Wagner was reaching up to cut a slice of ham.

"What do you do, Comrade?" I heard one of the flyers say to Al.

"Tanks."

"Tell me they aren't any good any more," said the flyer.

"Tell you a lot of things," Al said. "What you got there? Some dice?"

"Want to look at them?"

"No," said Al. "I want to handle them."

We went down the hall, Manolita, me and the tall Englishman, and found the boys had left already for the Gran Via restaurant. The Hungarian had stayed behind to replay the new discs. I was very hungry and the food at the Gran Via was lousy. The two who were making the film had already eaten and gone back to work on the bad camera.

This restaurant was in the basement and you had to pass a guard and go through the kitchen and down a stairs to get to it. It was a racket.

They had a millet and water soup, yellow rice with horse meat in it, and oranges for desert. There had been another dish of chickpeas with sausage in it that everybody said was terrible but it had run out. The newspaper men all sat at one table and the other tables were filled with officers and girls from Chicote's, people from the censorship, which was then in the telephone building across the street, and various unknown citizens.

The restaurant was run by an anarchist syndicate and they sold you wine that was all stamped with the label of the royal cellars and the date it had been put in the bins. Most of it was so old that it was either corked or just plain faded out and gone to pieces. You can't drink labels and I sent three bottles back as bad before we got a drinkable one. There was a row about this.

The waiters didn't know the different wines. They just brought you a bottle of wine and you took your chances. They were as different from the Chicote's waiters as black from white. These *bad waiter* waiters were all snotty, all over-tipped and they regularly had special dishes such as lobster or chicken that they sold extra for gigantic prices. But these had all been bought up before we got there so we just drew the soup, the rice and the oranges. The place always made me angry because the waiters were a crooked lot of profiteers and it was about as expensive to eat in, if you had one of the special dishes, as Twenty-One or the Colony in New York.

We were sitting at the table with a bottle of wine that just wasn't bad, you know you could taste it starting to go, but it wouldn't justify making a row about, when Al Wagner came in. He looked around the room, saw us and came over.

"What's the matter?" I said.

"They broke me," he said.

row over food for Al

"It didn't take very long."

"Not with those guys," he said. "That's a big game. What have they got to eat?"

I called a waiter over.

"It's too late," he said. "We can't serve anything now."

"This Comrade is in the tanks," I said. "He has fought all day and he will fight tomorrow and he hasn't eaten."

"That's not my fault," the waiter said. "It's too late. There isn't anything more. Why doesn't the Comrade eat with his unit? The army has plenty of food."

"I asked him to eat with me."

"You should have said something about it. It's too late now. We are not serving anything any more."

"Get the headwaiter."

The headwaiter said the cook had gone home and there was no fire in the kitchen. He went away. They were angry because we had sent the bad wine back.

"The hell with it," said Al. "Let's go somewhere else."

"There's no place you can eat at this hour. They've got food. I'll just have to go over and suck up to the headwaiter and give him some more money."

I went over and did just that and the sullen waiter brought a plate of cold sliced meats, then half a spiny lobster with mayonnaise, and a salad of lettuce and lentils. The headwaiter sold this out of his private stock which he was holding out either to take home, or sell to late comers.

"Cost you much?" Al asked.

"No," I lied.

"I'll bet it did," he said. "I'll fix up with you when I get paid."

"What do you get now?"

"I don't know yet. It was ten pesetas a day but they've raised it now I'm an officer. But we haven't got it yet and I haven't asked."

"Comrade," I called the waiter. He came over, still angry that the headwaiter had gone over his head and served Al. "Bring another bottle of wine please."

"What kind?"

"Any that is not too old so that the red is faded."

"It's all the same."

I said the equivalent of like hell it is in Spanish, and the waiter brought over a bottle of Château Mouton Rothschild 1906 that was just as good as the last claret we had was rotten.

"Boy that's wine," Al said. "What did you tell him to get that?"

"Nothing. He just made a lucky draw out of the bin."

"Most of that stuff from the palace stinks."

"It's too old. This is a hell of a climate on wine."

"There's that Wise Comrade," Al nodded across at another table.

The little man with the thick glasses that had talked to us about Largo Caballero was talking with some people I knew were very big shots indeed.

"I guess he's a big shot," I said.

"When they're high enough up they don't give a damn what they say. But I wish he would have waited until after tomorrow. It's kind of spoiled tomorrow for me."

I filled his glass.

"What he said sounded pretty sensible," Al went on. "I've been thinking it over. But my duty is to do what I'm ordered to do."

"Don't worry about it and get some sleep."

"I'm going to get in that game again if you'll let me take a thousand pesetas," Al said. "I've got a lot more than that coming to me and I'll give you an order on my pay."

"I don't want any order. You can pay me when you get it."

"I don't think I'm going to draw it," Al said. "I certainly sound wet, don't I? And I know gambling's bohemianism too. But in a game like that is the only time I don't think about tomorrow."

"Did you like that Manolita girl? She liked you."

"She's got eyes like a snake."

"She's not a bad girl. She's friendly and she's all right."

"I don't want any girl. I want to get back in that crap game."

Down the table Manolita was laughing at something the new Englishman had said in Spanish. Most of the people had left the table.

"Let's finish the wine and go," Al said. "Don't you want to get in that game?"

"I'll watch you for a while," I said and called the waiter over to bring us the bill.

"Where you go?" Manolita called down the table.

"To the room."

"We come by later on," she said. "This man is very funny."

"She is making most awful sport of me," the Englishman said. "She picks up my errors in Spanish. I say, doesn't *leche* mean milk?"

"That's one interpretation of it."

"*Does* it mean something beastly too?"

"I'm afraid so," I said.

"You know it *is* a beastly language," he said. "Now Manolita stop pulling my leg. I say stop it."

"I'm not pulling your leg," Manolita laughed. "I never touched your leg. I am just laughing about the *leche*."

"But it *does* mean milk. Didn't you just hear Edwin Henry say so?"

Manolita started to laugh again and we got up to go.

"He's a silly piece of work," Al said. "I'd almost like to take her away because he's so silly."

"You can never tell about an Englishman," I said. It was such a profound remark that I knew we had ordered too many bottles. Outside, in the street, it was turning cold and in the moonlight the clouds were passing very big and white across the wide, building-sided canyon of the Gran Via and we walked up the sidewalk with the day's fresh shell holes neatly cut in the cement, their rubble still not swept away, on up the rise of the hill toward the Plaza Callao where the Florida Hotel faced down the other little hill where the wide street ran that ended at the front.

We went past the two guards in the dark outside the door of the hotel and listened a minute in the doorway as the shooting down the street strengthened into a roll of firing then dropped off.

"If it keeps up I guess I ought to go down," Al said listening.

"That wasn't anything," I said. "Anyway that was off to the left by Carabanchel."

"It sounded straight down in the Campo."

"That's the way the sound throws here at night. It always fools you."

"They aren't going to counterattack us tonight," Al said. "When they've got those positions and we are up that creek they aren't going to leave their positions to try to kick us out of that creek."

"What creek?"

"You know the name of that creek."

"Oh. *That* creek."

"Yeah. Up that creek without a paddle."

"Come on inside. You didn't have to listen to that firing. That's the way it is every night."

We went inside, crossed the lobby, passing the night watchman at the concierge's desk and the night watchman got up and went with us to the elevator. He pushed a button and the elevator came down. In it was a man with a white curly sheep's wool jacket, the wool worn outside, a pink bald head, and a pink, angry face. He had six bottles of champagne under his arms and in his hands and he said, "What the hell's the idea of bringing the elevator down?"

"You've been riding in the elevator for an hour," the night watchman said.

"I can't help it," said the wooly jacket man. Then to me, "Where's Frank?"

"Frank who?"

"You know Frank," he said. "Come on help me with this elevator."

"You're drunk," I said to him. "Come on skip it and let us get upstairs."

"So would you be drunk," said the white woolly jacket man. "So would you be drunk Comrade old Comrade. Listen, where's Frank?"

"Where do you think he is?"

"In this fellow Henry's room where the crap game is."

"Come on with us," I said. "Don't fool with those buttons. That's why you stop it all the time."

"I can fly anything," said the woolly jacket man. "And I can fly this old elevator. Want me to stunt it?"

"Skip it," Al said to him. "You're drunk. We want to get to the crap game."

"Who are you? I'll hit you with a bottle full of champagne wine."

"Try it," said Al. "I'd like to cool you, you rummy fake Santa Claus."

"A rummy fake Santa Claus," said the bald man. "A rummy fake Santa Claus. And that's the thanks of the Republic."

We had gotten the elevator stopped at my floor and were walking down the hall. "Take some bottles," said the bald man. Then, "Do you know why I'm drunk?"

"No."

"Well I won't tell you. But you'd be surprised. A rummy fake Santa Claus. Well well well. What are you in Comrade?"

"Tanks."

"And you Comrade?"

"Making a picture."

"And I'm a rummy fake Santa Claus. Well. Well. Well. I repeat. Well. Well. Well."

"Go and drown in it," said Al. "You rummy fake Santa Claus."

We were outside the room now. The man in the white woolly coat took hold of Al's arm with his thumb and forefinger.

"You amuse me, Comrade," he said. "You truly amuse me."

I opened the door. The room was full of smoke and the game looked just as when we had left it except the ham was all gone off the table and the whisky all gone out of the bottle.

"It's Baldy," said one of the crap shooters.

"How do you do, Comrades," said Baldy bowing. "How do you do? How do you do? How do you do?"

The game broke up and they all started to shoot questions at him.

"I have made my report, Comrades," Baldy said. "And here is a little champagne wine. I am no longer interested in any but the picturesque aspects of the whole affair."

"Where did your wing men muck off to?"

"It wasn't their fault," said Baldy. "I was engaged in contemplating a terrific spectacle and I was ob-*livious* of the fact that I had any wing men until all of those Fiats started coming down over, past and under me and I realized that my trusty little air-o-plane no longer had any tail."

"Jees I wish you weren't drunk," said one of the flyers.

"But I *am* drunk," said Baldy. "And I hope all you gentlemen and Comrades will join me because I am very happy tonight even though I have been insulted by an ignorant tank man who has called me a rummy fake Santa Claus."

"I wish you were sober," the other flyer said. "How'd you get back to the field?"

"Don't ask me any questions," Baldy said with great dignity. "I returned in a staff car of the Twelfth Brigade. When I alighted with my trusty par-a-chute there was a tendency to regard me as a criminal fascist due to my inability to master the Lanish Spanguage. But all difficulties were smoothed away when I convinced them of my identity and I was treated with rare consideration. Oh boy you ought to have seen that Junker when she started to burn. That's what I was watching when the Fiats dove on me. Oh boy I wish I could tell you."

"He shot a tri-motor Junker down today over the Jarama and his wingmen mucked off on him and he got shot down and bailed out," one of the flyers said. "You know him. Baldy Jackson."

"How far did you drop before you pulled your rip cord Baldy?" asked another flyer.

"All of six thousand feet and I think my diaphragm is busted loose in front from when she came taut. I thought it would cut me in two. There must have been fifteen Fiats and I wanted to get completely clear. I had to fool with the chute plenty to get down on the right side of the river. I had to slip her plenty and I hit pretty hard. The wind was good."

"Frank had to go back to Alcalá," another flyer said. "We started a crap game. We got to get back there before daylight."

"I am in no mood to toy with the dice," said Baldy. "I am in a mood to drink champagne wine out of glasses with cigarette butts in them."

"I'll wash them," said Al.

"For Comrade Fake Santa Claus," said Baldy. "For old Comrade Claus."

"Skip it," said Al. He picked up the glasses and took them to the bathroom.

"Is he in the tanks?" asked one of the flyers.

"Yes. He's been there since the start."

"They tell me the tanks aren't any good anymore," a flyer said.

"You told him that once," I said. "Why don't you lay off? He's been working all day."

"So have we. But I mean really they aren't any good, are they?"

"Not so good. But he's good."

"I guess he's all right. He looks like a nice fellow. What kind of money do they make?"

"They got ten pesetas a day," I said. "Now he gets a lieutenant's pay."

"Spanish lieutenant?"

"Yes."

"I guess he's nuts all right. Or has he got politics?"

"He's got politics."

"Oh well," he said. "That explains it. Say Baldy you must have had a hell of a time bailing out with that wind pressure with the tail gone."

"Yes Comrade," said Baldy.

"How did you feel?"

"I was thinking all the time, Comrade."

"Baldy, how many bailed out of the Junker?"

"Four," said Baldy, "out of a crew of six. I was sure I'd killed the pilot. I noticed when he quit firing. There's a co-pilot that's a gunner too and I'm pretty sure I got him too. I must have because he quit firing too. But maybe it was the heat. Anyhow four came out. Would you like me to describe the scene? I can describe the scene very well."

He was sitting on the bed now with a large water glass of champagne in his hand and his pink head and pink face were moist with sweat.

"Why doesn't anyone drink to me?" asked Baldy. "I would like all comrades to drink to me and then, I will describe the scene in all its horror and its beauty."

We all drank.

"Where was I?" asked Baldy.

"Just coming out of the McAlester Hotel," a flyer said. "In all your horror and your beauty—don't clown, Baldy. Oddly enough we're interested."

"I will describe it," said Baldy. "But first I must have more champagne wine." He had drained the glass when we drank to him.

"If he drinks like that he'll go to sleep," another flyer said. "Only give him half a glass."

Baldy drank it off.

"I will describe it," he said. "After another little drink."

"Listen Baldy take it easy will you? This is something we want to get straight. You got no ship now for a few days but we're flying tomorrow and this is important as well as interesting."

"I made my report," said Baldy. "You can read it out at the field. They'll have a copy."

"Come on Baldy, snap out of it."

"I will describe it eventually," said Baldy. He shut and opened his eyes several times then said "Hello Comrade Santa Claus," to Al. "I will describe it eventually. All you Comrades have to do is listen."

And he described it.

"It was very strange and very beautiful," Baldy said and drank off the glass of champagne.

"Cut it out, Baldy," a flyer said.

"I have experienced profound emotions," Baldy said. "Highly profound emotions. Emotions of the deepest dye."

"Let's get back out to Alcalá," one flyer said. "That pink head isn't going to make sense. What about the game?"

"He's going to make sense," another flyer said. "He's just wind-ing up."

"Are you criticizing me?" asked Baldy. "Is *that* the thanks of the Republic?"

"Listen Santa Claus," Al said. "What was it like?"

"Are you asking me?" Baldy stared at him. "Are *you* putting questions to me? Have you ever been in action, Comrade?"

"No," said Al. "I got these eyebrows burnt off when I was shaving."

"Keep your drawers on, Comrade," said Baldy. "I will describe the strange and beautiful scene. I'm a writer you know as well as a flyer."

He nodded his head in confirmation of his own statement.

"He writes for the Meridian, Mississippi *Argus*," said a flyer. "All the time. They can't stop him."

"I have talent as a writer," said Baldy. "I have a fresh and original talent for description. I have a newspaper clipping which I have lost which says so. Now I will launch myself on the de-scription."

"O.K. What did it look like?"

"Comrades," said Baldy. "You can't describe it." He held out his glass.

"What did I tell you?" said a flyer. "He couldn't make sense in a month. He never could make sense."

"You," said Baldy, "you unfortunate little fellow. All right. When I banked out of it I looked down and of course she had been pouring back smoke but she was holding right on her course to get over the mountains. She was losing altitude fast and I came up and over and dove on her again. There were still wingmen then and she'd lurched and started to smoke twice as much and then the door of the cockpit came open and it was just like looking into a blast furnace, and then they started to come out. I'd half rolled, dove, and then pulled up out of it and I was looking back and down and they were coming out of her, out through the blast furnace door, dropping out trying to get clear, and the chutes opened up and they looked like great big beautiful morning glories opening up and she was just one big thing of flame now like you never saw and going round and round and there were four chutes just as beautiful as anything

you could see just pulling slow against the sky and then one
started to burn at the edge and as it burned the man started to
drop fast and I was watching him when the bullets started to come
by and the Fiats right behind them and the bullets and the
Fiats."

"You're a writer all right," said one flyer. "You ought to write
for *War Aces*. Do you mind telling me in plain language what
happened?"

"No," said Baldy. "I'll tell you. But you know, no kidding, it
was something to see. And I never shot down any big tri-motor
Junkers before and I'm happy."

"Everybody's happy, Baldy. Tell us what happened, really."

"O.K.," said Baldy. "I'll just drink a little wine and then I'll
tell you."

"How were you when you sighted them?"

"We were in a left echelon of V's. Then we went into a left
echelon of echelons and dove onto them with all four guns until
you could have touched them before we rolled out of it. We
crippled three others. The Fiats were hanging up in the sun.
They didn't come down until I was sightseeing all by myself."

"Did your wing men muck off?"

"No. It was my fault I started watching the spectacle and they
were gone. There isn't any formation for watching spectacles. I
guess they went on and picked up the echelon. I don't know.
Don't ask me. And I'm tired. I was elated. But now I'm tired."

"You're sleepy you mean. You're rum-dumb and sleepy."

"I am simply tired," said Baldy. "A man in my position has the
right to be tired. And if I become sleepy I have the right to be
sleepy. Don't I Santa Claus?" he said to Al.

"Yeah," said Al. "I guess you have the right to be sleepy. I'm
even sleepy myself. Isn't there going to be any crap game?"

"We got to get him out to Alcalá and we've got to get out
there too," a flyer said. "Why? You lost money in the game?"

"A little," said Al.

"You want to try to pass for it once?" the flyer asked him.

"I'll shoot a thousand," Al said.

"I'll fade you," the flyer said. "You guys don't make much do
you?"

"No," said Al. "We don't make much."

He laid the thousand peseta note down on the floor, rolled the dice between his palms so they clicked over and over, and shot them out on the floor with a snap. Two ones showed.

"They're still your dice," the flyer said picking up the bill and looking at Al.

"I don't need them," said Al. He stood up.

"Need any dough?" the flyer asked him. Looking at him curiously.

"Got no use for it," Al said.

"We've got to get the hell out to Alcalá," the flyer said. "We'll have a game some night soon. We'll get hold of Frank and the rest of them. We could get up a pretty good game. Can we give you a lift?"

"Yes. Want a ride?"

"No," Al said. "I'm walking. It's just down the street."

"Well we're going out to Alcalá. Does anybody know the password for tonight?"

"Oh the chauffeur will have it. He'll have gone by and picked it up before dark."

"Come on Baldy. You drunken sleepy bum."

"Not me," said Baldy. "I am a potential ace of the people's army."

"Takes ten to be an ace. Even if you count Italians. You've only got one, Baldy."

"It wasn't Italians," said Baldy. "It was Germans. And you didn't see her when she was all hot like that inside. She was a raging inferno."

"Carry him out," said a flyer. "He's writing for that Meridian, Mississippi paper again. Well so long. Thanks for having us up in the room."

They all shook hands and they were gone. I went to the head of the stairs with them. The elevator was no longer running and I watched them go down the stairs. One was on each side of Baldy and he was nodding his head slowly. He was really sleepy now.

In their room the two I was working on the picture with were still working over the bad camera. It was delicate, eye-straining work and when I asked, "Do you think you'll get her?" the tall one said, "Yes. Sure. We have to. I make a piece now which was broken."

"What was the party?" asked the other. "We work always on this damn camera."

"American flyers," I said. "And a fellow I used to know who's in tanks."

"Goot fun? I am sorry not to be there."

"All right," I said. "Kind of funny."

"You must get sleep. We must all be up early. We must be fresh for tomorrow."

"How much more have you got on that camera?"

"There it goes again. Damn such shape springs."

"Leave him alone. We finish it then we all sleep. What time you call us?"

"Five?"

"All right. As soon as is light."

"Good night."

"Salud. Get some sleep."

"Salud," I said. "We've got to be closer tomorrow."

"Yes," he said. "I have thought so too. Much closer. I am glad you know."

Al was asleep in the big chair in the room with the light on his face. I put a blanket over him but he woke.

"I'm going down."

"Sleep here. I'll set the alarm and call you."

"Something might happen with the alarm," he said. "I better go down. I don't want to get there late."

"I'm sorry about the game."

"They'd have broke me anyway," he said. "Those guys are poisonous with dice."

"You had the dice there on that last play."

"They're poisonous fading you too. They're strange guys too. I guess they don't get overpaid. I guess if you are doing it for dough there isn't enough dough to pay for doing it."

"Want me to walk down with you?"

"No," he said, standing up, and buckling on the big web-belted Colt he had taken off when he came back after dinner to the game. "No, I feel fine now. I've got my perspective back again. All you need is a perspective."

"I'd like to walk down."

"No. Get some sleep. I'll go down and I'll get a good five hours sleep before it starts."

"That early?"

"Yeah. You won't have any light to film by. You might as well stay in bed." He took an envelope out of his leather coat and laid it on the table. "Take this stuff will you and send it to my brother in N.Y. His address is on the back of the envelope."

"Sure. But I won't have to send it."

"No," he said. "I don't think you will now. But there's some pictures and stuff they'll like to have. He's got a nice wife. Want to see her picture?"

He took it out of his pocket. It was inside his identity book. It showed a pretty, dark girl standing by a rowboat on the shore of a lake.

"Up in the Catskills," said Al. "Yeah. He's got a nice wife. She's a Jewish girl. Yes," he said. "Don't let me get wet again. So long, kid. Take it easy. I tell you truly I feel O.K. now. And I didn't feel good when I came out this afternoon."

"Let me walk down."

"No. You might have trouble coming back through the Plaza de España. Some of those guys are nervous at night. Good night. See you tomorrow night."

"That's the way to talk."

Upstairs in the room above mine, Manolita and the Englishman were making quite a lot of noise. So she evidently hadn't been arrested.

"That's right. That's the way to talk," Al said. "Takes you sometimes three or four hours to get so you can do it though."

He'd put the leather helmet on now with the raised padded ridge and his face looked dark and I noticed the dark hollows under his eyes.

"See you tomorrow night at Chicote's," I said.

"That's right," he said, and wouldn't look me in the eye. "See you tomorrow night at Chicote's."

"What time?"

"Listen, that's enough," he said. "Tomorrow night at Chicote's. We don't have to go into the time." And he went out.

If you hadn't known him pretty well and if you hadn't seen the terrain where he was going to attack tomorrow, you would have thought he was very angry about something. I guess somewhere inside of himself he was angry, very angry. You get angry about a lot of things and you, yourself, dying uselessly is one of them. But then I guess angry is about the best way that you can be when you attack.

Composed Feb, 1939
Pub, Cosmopolitan, Oct, 1939

Under the Ridge

In the heat of the day with the dust blowing, we came back, dry-mouthed, nose-clogged and heavy-loaded, down out of the battle to the long ridge above the river where the Spanish troops lay in reserve.

I sat down with my back against the shallow trench, my shoulders and the back of my head against the earth, clear now from even stray bullets, and looked at what lay below us in the hollow. There was the tank reserve, the tanks covered with branches chopped from olive trees. To their left were the staff cars, mud-daubed and branch-covered, and between the two a long line of men carrying stretchers wound down through the gap to where, on the flat at the foot of the ridge, ambulances were loading. Commissary mules loaded with sacks of bread and kegs of wine, and a train of ammunition mules, led by their drivers, were coming up the gap in the ridge, and men with empty stretchers were walking slowly up the trail with the mules.

To the right, below the curve of the ridge, I could see the entrance to the cave where the brigade staff was working, and their signaling wires ran out of the top of the cave and curved on over the ridge in the shelter of which we lay.

Motorcyclists in leather suits and helmets came up and down the cut on their cycles or, where it was too steep, walking them, and leaving them beside the cut, walked over to the entrance to the cave and ducked inside. As I watched, a big Hungarian cyclist that I knew came out of the cave, tucked some papers in his leather wallet, walked over to his motorcycle and, pushing it up through the stream of mules and stretcher-bearers, threw a leg over the saddle and roared on over the ridge, his machine churning a storm of dust.

Other Stories

"An African Story"

"Get a Seeing-eyed Dog"

"A Man of the World"

Spanish Civil War

1) "Capital of the World" (38)

2) "Old Man at the Bridge" (78)

---

3) "The Denunciation" (89)

4) "The Butterfly & the Tank" (101)

5) "Night Before Battle" (110)

6) "Under the Ridge" (140)

7) "Nobody Ever Dies" (xerox)

Below, across the flat where the ambulances were coming and going, was the green foliage that marked the line of the river. There was a large house with a red tile roof and there was a gray stone mill, and from the trees around the big house beyond the river came the flashes of our guns. They were firing straight at us and there were the twin flashes, then the throaty, short *bung-bung* of the three-inch pieces and then the rising cry of the shells coming toward us and going on over our heads. As always, we were short of artillery. There were only four batteries down there, when there should have been forty, and they were firing only two guns at a time. The attack had failed before we came down.

"Are you Russians?" a Spanish soldier asked me.

"No, Americans," I said. "Have you any water?"

"Yes, comrade." He handed over a pigskin bag. These troops in reserve were soldiers only in name and from the fact that they were in uniform. They were not intended to be used in the attack, and they sprawled along this line under the crest of the ridge, huddled in groups, eating, drinking and talking, or simply sitting dumbly, waiting. The attack was being made by an International Brigade.

We both drank. The water tasted of asphalt and pig bristles.

"Wine is better," the soldier said. "I will get wine."

"Yes. But for the thirst, water."

"There is no thirst like the thirst of battle. Even here, in reserve, I have much thirst."

"That is fear," said another soldier. "Thirst is fear."

"No," said another. "With fear there is thirst, always. But in battle there is much thirst even when there is no fear."

"There is always fear in battle," said the first soldier.

"For you," said the second soldier.

"It is normal," the first soldier said.

"For you."

"Shut your dirty mouth," said the first soldier. "I am simply a man who tells the truth."

It was a bright April day and the wind was blowing wildly so that each mule that came up the gap raised a cloud of dust, and the two men at the ends of a stretcher each raised a cloud of dust that blew together and made one, and below, across the flat, long streams of dust moved out from the ambulances and blew away in the wind.

I felt quite sure I was not going to be killed on that day now, since we had done our work well in the morning, and twice during the early part of the attack we should have been killed and were not; and this had given me confidence. The first time had been when we had gone up with the tanks and picked a place from which to film the attack. Later I had a sudden distrust for the place and we had moved the cameras about two hundred yards to the left. Just before leaving, I had marked the place in quite the oldest way there is of marking a place, and within ten minutes a six-inch shell had lit on the exact place where I had been and there was no trace of any human being ever having been there. Instead, there was a large and clearly blasted hole in the earth.

Then, two hours later, a Polish officer, recently detached from the battalion and attached to the staff, had offered to show us the positions the Poles had just captured and, coming from under the lee of a fold of hill, we had walked into machine-gun fire that we had to crawl out from under with our chins tight to the ground and dust in our noses, and at the same time made the sad discovery that the Poles had captured no positions at all that day but were a little further back than the place they had started from. And now, lying in the shelter of the trench, I was wet with sweat, hungry and thirsty and hollow inside from the now-finished danger of the attack.

"You are sure you are not Russians?" asked a soldier. "There are Russians here today."

"Yes. But we are not Russians."

"You have the face of a Russian."

"No," I said. "You are wrong, comrade. l have quite a funny face but it is not the face of a Russian."

"He has the face of a Russian," pointing at the other one of us who was working on a camera.

"Perhaps. But still he is not Russian. Where you from?"

"Extremadura," he said proudly.

"Are there any Russians in Extremadura?" I asked.

"No," he told me, even more proudly. "There are no Russians in Extremadura, and there are no Extremadurans in Russia."

"What are your politics?"

"I hate all foreigners," he said.

"That's a broad political program."

"I hate the Moors, the English, the French, the Italians, the Germans, the North Americans and the Russians."

"You hate them in that order?"

"Yes. But perhaps I hate the Russians the most."

"Man, you have very interesting ideas," I said. "Are you a Fascist?"

"No. I am an Extremaduran and I hate foreigners."

"He has very rare ideas," said another soldier. "Do not give him too much importance. Me, I like foreigners. I am from Valencia. Take another cup of wine, please."

I reached up and took the cup, the other wine still brassy in my mouth. I looked at the Extremaduran. He was tall and thin. His face was haggard and unshaven, and his cheeks were sunken. He stood straight up in his rage, his blanket cape around his shoulders.

"Keep your head down," I told him. "There are many lost bullets coming over."

"I have no fear of bullets and I hate all foreigners," he said fiercely.

"You don't have to fear bullets," I said, "but you should avoid them when you are in reserve. It is not intelligent to be wounded when it can be avoided."

"I am not afraid of anything," the Extremaduran said.

"You are very lucky, comrade."

"It's true," the other, with the wine cup, said. "He has no fear, not even of the *aviones*."

"He is crazy," another soldier said. "Everyone fears planes. They kill little but make much fear."

"I have no fear. Neither of planes nor of nothing," the Extremaduran said. "And I hate every foreigner alive."

Down the gap, walking beside two stretcher-bearers and seeming to pay no attention at all to where he was, came a tall man in International Brigade uniform with a blanket rolled over his shoulder and tied at his waist. His head was held high and he looked like a man walking in his sleep. He was middle-aged. He was not carrying a rifle and, from where I lay, he did not look wounded.

I watched him walking alone down out of the war. Before he came to the staff cars he turned to the left and his head still held high in that strange way, he walked over the edge of the ridge and out of sight.

The one who was with me, busy changing film in the hand cameras, had not noticed him.

A single shell came in over the ridge and fountained in dirt and black smoke just short of the tank reserve.

Someone put his head out of the cave where Brigade headquarters was and then disappeared inside. I thought it looked like a good place to go, but knew they would all be furious in there because the attack was a failure, and I did not want to face them. If an operation was successful they were happy to have motion pictures of it. But if it was a failure everyone was in such a rage there was always a chance of being sent back under arrest.

"They may shell us now," I said.

"That makes no difference to me," said the Extremaduran. I was beginning to be a little tired of the Extremaduran.

"Have you any more wine to spare?" I asked. My mouth was still dry.

"Yes, man. There are gallons of it," the friendly soldier said. He was short, big-fisted and very dirty, with a stubble of beard about the same length as the hair on his cropped head. "Do you think they will shell us now?"

"They should," I said. "But in this war you can never tell."

"What is the matter with this war?" asked the Extremaduran angrily. "Don't you like this war?"

"Shut up!" said the friendly soldier. "I command here, and these comrades are our guests."

"Then let him not talk against our war," said the Extremaduran. "No foreigners shall come here and talk against our war."

"What town are you from, comrade?" I asked the Extremaduran.

"Badajoz," he said. "I am from Badajoz. In Badajoz, we have been sacked and pillaged and our women violated by the English, the French and now the Moors. What the Moors have done now is no worse than what the English did under Wellington. You should read history. My great-grandmother was killed by the English. The house where my family lived was burned by the English."

"I regret it," I said. "Why do you hate the North Americans?"

"My father was killed by the North Americans in Cuba while he was there as a conscript."

"I am sorry for that, too. Truly sorry. Believe me. And why do you hate the Russians?"

"Because they are the representatives of tyranny and I hate their faces. You have the face of a Russian."

"Maybe we better get out of here," I said to the one who was with me and who did not speak Spanish. "It seems I have the face of a Russian and it's getting me into trouble."

"I'm going to sleep," he said. "This is a good place. Don't talk so much and you won't get into trouble."

"There's a comrade here that doesn't like me. I think he's an anarchist."

"Well, watch out he doesn't shoot you, then. I'm going to sleep."

Just then two men in leather coats, one short and stocky, the other of medium height, both with civilian caps, flat, high-cheek-boned faces, wooden-holstered Mauser pistols strapped to their legs, came out of the gap and headed toward us.

The taller of them spoke to me in French. "Have you seen a French comrade pass through here?" he asked. "A comrade with a blanket tied around his shoulders in the form of a bandoleer? A comrade of about forty-five or fifty years old? Have you seen such a comrade going in the direction away from the front?"

"No," I said. "I have not seen such a comrade." [lie]

He looked at me a moment and I noticed his eyes were a grayish-yellow and that they did not blink at all.

"Thank you, comrade," he said, in his odd French, and then spoke rapidly to the other man with him in a language I did not understand. They went off and climbed the highest part of the ridge, from where they could see down all the gullies.

"There is the true face of Russians," the Extremaduran said.

"Shut up!" I said. I was watching the two men in the leather coats. They were standing there, under considerable fire, looking carefully over all the broken country below the ridge and toward the river.

Suddenly one of them saw what he was looking for, and pointed. Then the two started to run like hunting dogs, one straight down over the ridge, the other at an angle as though to cut someone off. Before the second one went over the crest I could see him drawing his pistol and holding it ahead of him as he ran.

"And how do you like that?" asked the Extremaduran.

"No better than you," I said.

Over the crest of the parallel ridge I heard the Mausers' jerky barking. They kept it up for more than a dozen shots. They must have opened fire at too long a range. After all the burst of shooting there was a pause and then a single shot.

The Extremaduran looked at me sullenly and said nothing. I thought it would be simpler if the shelling started. But it did not start.

The two in the leather coats and civilian caps came back over the ridge, walking together, and then down to the gap, walking downhill with that odd bent-kneed way of the two-legged animal coming down a steep slope. They turned up the gap as a tank came whirring and clanking down and moved to one side to let it pass. The tanks had failed again that day, and the drivers coming down from the lines in their leather helmets, the tank turrets open now as they came into the shelter of the ridge, had the straight-ahead stare of football players who have been removed from a game for yellowness.

The two flat-faced men in the leather coats stood by us on the ridge to let the tank pass.

"Did you find the comrade you were looking for?" I asked the taller one of them in French.

"Yes, comrade. Thank you," he said and looked me over very carefully.

"What does he say?" the Extremaduran asked.

"He says they found the comrade they were looking for," I told him. The Extremaduran said nothing.

We had been all that morning in the place the middle-aged Frenchman had walked out of. We had been there in the dust, the smoke, the noise, the receiving of wounds, the death, the fear of death, the bravery, the cowardice, the insanity and failure of an unsuccessful attack. We had been there on that plowed field men could not cross and live. You dropped and lay flat; making a mound to shield your head; working your chin into the dirt; waiting for the order to go up that slope no man could go up and live.

We had been with those who lay there waiting for the tanks that did not come; waiting under the inrushing shriek and roaring crash of the shelling; the metal and the earth thrown like clods from a dirt fountain; and overhead the cracking, whispering fire like a curtain. We knew how those felt, waiting. They were as far forward as they could get. And men could not move further and live, when the order came to move ahead.

We had been there all morning in the place the middle-aged Frenchman had come walking away from. I understood how a man might suddenly, seeing clearly the stupidity of dying in an unsuccessful attack; or suddenly seeing it clearly, as you can see clearly and justly before you die; seeing its hopelessness, seeing its idiocy, seeing how it really was, simply get back and walk away from it as the Frenchman had done. He could walk out of it not from cowardice, but simply from seeing too clearly; knowing suddenly that he had to leave it; knowing there was no other thing to do.

The Frenchman had come walking out of the attack with great dignity and I understood him as a man. But, as a soldier, these other men who policed the battle had hunted him down, and the death he had walked away from had found him when he was just over the ridge, clear of the bullets and the shelling, and walking toward the river.

"And that," the Extremaduran said to me, nodding toward the battle police.

"Is war," I said. "In war, it is necessary to have discipline."

"And to live under that sort of discipline we should die?"

"Without discipline everyone will die anyway."

"There is one kind of discipline and another kind of discipline," the Extremaduran said. "Listen to me. In February we were here where we are now and the Fascists attacked. They drove us from the hills that you Internationals tried to take today and that you could not take. We fell back to here; to this ridge. Internationals came up and took the line ahead of us."

"I know that," I said.

"But you do not know this," he went on angrily. "There was a boy from my province who became frightened during the bombardment, and he shot himself in the hand so that he could leave the line because he was afraid."

The other soldiers were all listening now. Several nodded.

"Such people have their wounds dressed and are returned at once to the line," the Extremaduran went on. "It is just."

"Yes," I said. "That is as it should be."

"That is as it should be," said the Extremaduran. "But this boy shot himself so badly that the bone was all smashed and there surged up an infection and his hand was amputated."

Several soldiers nodded.

"Go on, tell him the rest," said one.

"It might be better not to speak of it," said the cropped-headed, bristly-faced man who said he was in command.

"It is my duty to speak," the Extremaduran said.

The one in command shrugged his shoulders. "I did not like it either," he said. "Go on, then. But I do not like to hear it spoken of either."

"This boy remained in the hospital in the valley since February," the Extremaduran said. "Some of us have seen him in the hospital. All say he was well liked in the hospital and made himself as useful as a man with one hand can be useful. Never was he under arrest. Never was there anything to prepare him."

The man in command handed me the cup of wine again without saying anything. They were all listening; as men who cannot read or write listen to a story.

"Yesterday, at the close of day, before we knew there was to be an attack. Yesterday, before the sun set, when we thought today was to be as any other day, they brought him up the trail in the gap there from the flat. We were cooking the evening meal and they brought him up. There were only four of them. Him, the boy Paco, those two you have just seen in the leather coats and the caps, and an officer from the Brigade. We saw the four of them climbing together up the gap, and we saw Paco's hands were not tied, nor was he bound in any way.

"When we saw him we all crowded around and said, 'Hello,

Paco. How are you, Paco? How is everything, Paco, old boy, old Paco?'

"Then he said, 'Everything's all right. Everything is good except this'—and showed us the stump.

"Paco said, 'That was a cowardly and foolish thing. I am sorry that I did that thing. But I try to be useful with one hand. I will do what I can with one hand for the Cause.'"

"Yes," interrupted a soldier. "He said that. I heard him say that."

"We spoke with him," the Extremaduran said. "And he spoke with us. When such people with the leather coats and the pistols come it is always a bad omen in a war, as is the arrival of people with map cases and field glasses. Still we thought they had brought him for a visit, and all of us who had not been to the hospital were happy to see him, and as I say, it was the hour of the evening meal and the evening was clear and warm."

"This wind only rose during the night," a soldier said.

"Then," the Extremaduran went on somberly, "one of *them* said to the officer in Spanish, 'Where is the place?'

"'Where is the place this Paco was wounded?' asked the officer."

"I answered him," said the man in command. "I showed the place. It is a little further down than where you are."

"Here is the place," said a soldier. He pointed, and I could see it was the place. It showed clearly that it was the place.

"Then one of them led Paco by the arm to the place and held him there by the arm while the other spoke in Spanish. He spoke in Spanish, making many mistakes in the language. At first we wanted to laugh, and Paco started to smile. I could not understand all the speech, but it was that Paco must be punished as an example, in order that there would be no more self-inflicted wounds, and that all others would be punished in the same way.

"Then, while the one held Paco by the arm; Paco, looking very ashamed to be spoken of this way when he was already ashamed and sorry; the other took his pistol out and shot Paco in the back of the head without any word to Paco. Nor any word more."

The soldiers all nodded.

"It was thus," said one. "You can see the place. He fell with his mouth there. You can see it."

I had seen the place clearly enough from where I lay.

"He had no warning and no chance to prepare himself," the one in command said. "It was very brutal."

"It is for this that I now hate Russians as well as all other foreigners," said the Extremaduran. "We can give ourselves no illusions about foreigners. If you are a foreigner, I am sorry. But for myself, now, I can make no exceptions. You have eaten bread and drunk wine with us. Now I think you should go."

"Do not speak in that way," the man in command said to the Extremaduran. "It is necessary to be formal."

"I think we had better go," I said.

"You are not angry?" the man in command said. "You can stay in this shelter as long as you wish. Are you thirsty? Do you wish more wine?"

"Thank you very much," I said. "I think we had better go."

"You understand my hatred?" asked the Extremaduran.

"I understand your hatred," I said.

"Good," he said and put out his hand. "I do not refuse to shake hands. And that you, personally, have much luck."

"Equally to you," I said. "Personally, and as a Spaniard."

I woke the one who took the pictures and we started down the ridge toward Brigade headquarters. The tanks were all coming back now and you could hardly hear yourself talk for the noise.

"Were you talking all that time?"

"Listening."

"Hear anything interesting?"

"Plenty."

"What do you want to do now?"

"Get back to Madrid."

"We should see the General."

"Yes," I said. "We must."

The General was coldly furious. He had been ordered to make the attack as a surprise with one brigade only, bringing everything up before daylight. It should have been made by at least a division. He had used three battalions and held one in reserve. The French tank commander had got drunk to be brave for the attack and finally was too drunk to function. He was to be shot when he sobered up.

The tanks had not come up in time and finally had refused to advance, and two of the battalions had failed to attain their objectives. The third had taken theirs, but it formed an untenable salient. The only real result had been a few prisoners, and these had been confided to the tank men to bring back and the tank men had killed them. The General had only failure to show, and they had killed his prisoners.

"What can I write on it?" I asked.

"Nothing that is not in the official communiqué. Have you any whisky in that long flask?"

"Yes."

He took a drink and licked his lips carefully. He had once been a captain of Hungarian Hussars, and he had once captured a gold train in Siberia when he was a leader of irregular cavalry with the Red Army and held it all one winter when the thermometer went down to forty below zero. We were good friends and he loved whisky, and he is now dead.

"Get out of here now," he said. "Have you transport?"

"Yes."

"Did you get any pictures?"

"Some. The tanks."

"The tanks," he said bitterly. "The swine. The cowards. Watch out you don't get killed," he said. "You are supposed to be a writer."

"I can't write now."

"Write it afterwards. You can write it all afterwards. And don't get killed. Especially, don't get killed. Now, get out of here."

He could not take his own advice because he was killed two months later. But the oddest thing about that day was how marvelously the pictures we took of the tanks came out. On the screen they advanced over the hill irresistibly, mounting the crests like great ships, to crawl clanking on toward the illusion of victory we screened.

The nearest any man was to victory that day was probably the Frenchman who came, with his head held high, walking out of the battle. But his victory only lasted until he had walked halfway down the ridge. We saw him lying stretched out there on the slope of the ridge, still wearing his blanket, as we came walking down the cut to get into the staff car that would take us to Madrid.